SHADOWSPELL ACADEMY

YEAR OF THE CHAMELEON, BOOK 5

SHANNON MAYER

www.shannonmayer.com

CONTENTS

ACKNOWLEDGMENTS

Could not have done this without my own amazing Crew around me, reminding me that no matter how hard some parts of the story are, there's always a way through if you lean on your friends. Thank you.

1

WILD

I would have preferred it if he'd knocked me out. Instead, the Shadowkiller's spell had frozen me, making it so I could see, and hear, and think but not act. So I couldn't do a damn thing about him slinging me over his shoulder like I was a bag of feed. My friends were under attack as he hauled me away, and I could do nothing to help them. I couldn't so much as twitch a muscle or blink my eyes. All I could do was watch what was unfolding in front of me.

Yeah, it would have been kinder if he'd made me truly oblivious to what was happening.

Kindness, though, did not appear to be in the Shadowkiller's repertoire.

"The SUV is waiting," the gargoyle Ash said,

his wings blocking my vision for a moment. He'd been my professor for about 3.2 seconds, and it turned out he was working with the Shadowkiller, my uncle (gah, that still galled), all along. Helping Uncle Nicholas get close to me through him, making me believe that he was my friend.

In the distance, my real friends called out to me. One voice was missing, though. Colt. My guts twisted and a groan slipped out of me. He'd been killed because I'd let him into my crew. Killed trying to protect me. A shudder rippled and I struggled to breathe, not because of the spell, but because of my damn emotions.

I had to get myself under control. I had to lock all that up . . . *I'm sorry, Colt. I have to put you aside. For now.* I'd hurt later for my friend. But not now, not in the middle of a fight for our lives.

Wally's voice rose over the others as she demanded that the Shadowkiller put me down.

"DON'T YOU DARE TAKE HER!" SHE YELLED, AND MY heart swelled a little. She was a good friend, more loyal than most. No, that wasn't true. All my friends here were like her. Good. Loyal. Stronger than they realized.

Despite that, they were no match for the Shadowkiller, any more than I was apparently.

Explosions rocketed around us, filling the air with dust and debris, rumbling against my chest, but I couldn't move no matter how hard I tried, and I *was* trying. My breath came in ragged gulps as my adrenaline soared and my internal warning system went off the rails, screaming at me to run, to fight, to do something.

"Stop struggling, Maribel," Nicholas said, his voice calm and as smooth as butter on a hot Texas day. He adjusted his hold on me, and a wave of darkness threatened at the edge of my vision.

"Not. My. Name." It was all I could do to say those three words and stay conscious. Sweat broke out across my face and dripped down my cheeks to the floor below. Three words and I was exhausted, wrung out from the effort.

I blinked and behind us stood Tommy. My brother's ghost was shaking his head, one hand in his hair as he stared at me. How could I see him? I wasn't touching Wally. That was the connection I needed in order to see ghosts.

There was movement off to my left, drawing my eyes as that was all I could move. The pebbled skin of Ash blocked my view as Nicholas strode toward the front doors of the House of Wonder. He almost had me out.

"Fight!" Tommy yelled at me. I wanted to yell back that I was trying. A groan was all I managed.

"Ethan, stop him!" Wally screamed, and a spell slammed the doors shut. My uncle—God, I did not want to think of being related to this monster—just flicked his wand and the doors ripped open, snapping at the hinges as they spun away.

As if Ethan's magic was nothing to him.

Another explosion ripped out behind us, and the ground shook as the building was rocked from the inside.

They—Ash and the Shadowkiller—had set bombs off in the House of Wonder. Just like they'd done to the other houses.

"That should slow them down," Ash said with more than a little satisfaction. I wouldn't have pegged him for bloodthirsty, but here it was—the truth. He'd fooled me. Damn it, where had my internal warning system been when I'd met the gargoyle? Maybe it had still been dampened by the spell the mages had set on all of us upon our arrival. A spell to keep us slow and compliant while we were in the House of Wonder.

The honk of vehicles blitzed through the

booms behind us from the explosives that had gone off. There was a screech of tires, and then the world turned upside down and I was staring at the night sky for a split second as I was flipped into the back seat of what looked like a black SUV or maybe a truck. Hard to say from that angle.

"Original." I bit out the word, face down on the leather seats, my jaw cramping as if I'd been kicked in the face by a donkey. The spell the Shadowkiller had wrapped around me tightened, reminding me of the python that had attacked us the morning after Ruby's assault on me. Even as I thought it, there was a shimmer of scales around me.

"Snake." I bit that word out too, putting the pieces together.

"Yes, that was me," Nicholas said slowly. "I can see the questions in your mind, Maribel. That's the power of a family connection in our world when we are close in proximity, if you know how to use it, of course. And, yes, I sent that snake to wrap you up and bring you back to me. Separating you from your friends was the key. That older student, the Shade, didn't realize the python was out of the ordinary—mind you, it is something the House of Wonder uses for training." He sighed. "Truly, this is not how I wanted things to go. But such is life, rarely bending to your will the way you'd like it to. We have to hurry, Ash. I've only got so much time before . . ." He rubbed his temple.

Before what? He didn't finish his sentence, leaving me to wonder.

Before he drained my life?

Before another bomb exploded?

"The spell will cover us for another few hours at best," Ash said.

Nicholas settled into his seat next to me and put on a seat belt with a click. Like . . . a normal person. Not a damn crazy killer of so many of the people in our world. "Ash, let's go," he said. "There is nothing here. Except for Maribel, this night is a complete bust."

"Could it be hidden better than we thought?" Ash asked.

Nicholas sighed. "I don't know. I was certain . . . and yet there was nothing." My eyes couldn't physically see him, but I saw him clearly in my mind's eye. He was again rubbing at his face, looking out the window. What the freaking damn hell was this? That family connection he was talking about?

"Five of them, all missing," Ash said as he drove us through the city. "You'd think in all these years, there would be at least one found. But only whispers."

"I believe one was," Nicholas said. "And then lost again. Lexi was close . . ."

What the hell were they talking about? What were they searching for and why was my mother's name involved? I had to get out of here, no matter that they were giving me information that sounded interesting, and possibly useful.

I'd take freedom over knowledge at that point, a thousand times over.

But every second I struggled against the spell, it strangled me until I could see the patterns of the snake wrapped around me, constricting me tighter and tighter until my vision spotted with stars and I gasped for breath.

"You're going to pass out soon if you keep that up," Professor Ash said from the front of the SUV. I couldn't see him, either, but I could hear him clearly.

Another wave of self-recrimination washed over me. I should have suspected something was up the moment he said *Nicholas* had been one of his favorite students, that he wasn't what people believed him to be. Shoulda coulda woulda.

But I'd been too busy dealing with Ruby's

attack on me, the sickness spreading through the House of Wonder, and trying to stay alive as the Sandman trained me with fists and feet to pay attention to what was going on around me.

The Sandman.

Shit, he had a connection to me through the pendant I wore to mark me as a Shade.

A pendant that was no longer with me, but maybe . . . I closed my eyes and let out a slow breath, and the constriction eased around my chest. Another slow breath, and I focused all my mental energy on a shout.

CAN YOU HEAR ME?

Professor Ash gave a low grunt and his leathery wings rustled. "He cannot hear you, though I can. I have replaced myself as the one who can track you."

My eyes flew open, and I twisted into a more upright sitting position before the spell clamped down on my arms and legs again, freezing me in place once more. My uncle calmly leaned over and buckled me in, as if he was bringing me to the park to pitch balls.

Questions pinged through my head, not least among them where they were taking me, whether they planned to kill me, and who'd killed Tommy.

Which meant I couldn't slump into a pile of goo. I had to be aware.

Professor Ash twisted around in the front passenger seat to face me, his eyes full of intelligence. He wasn't the one driving, then. I considered checking, but I couldn't look away from the gargoyle.

"There are many questions rolling through you. Focus on one, and I will do my best to answer. You need to understand that there are some things I cannot answer because of my loyalties and the ties that bind me to them," Ash dipped his head toward my left, where the Shadowkiller sat. "But I will share with you what I can."

My *uncle* said nothing, his body still except for one hand tapping away rapidly on his leg, a staccato beat.

I didn't close my eyes, but went through the list of questions quickly, settling on the most obvious.

Are you two going to kill me?

The professor shook his head. "No, your death is not the plan, not in the least. There is much to discuss, and very little time in which to do so."

Not in the plan? That meant it could happen though.

The SUV took a sharp left, which tipped me to

the side and changed my field of vision as the vehicle picked up speed once more. I couldn't see who was driving, and even if I'd been able to turn my head more, I wouldn't have been able to. There was a partial plexi-glass partition between the front and back seats on that side, and it was shaded out between me and the driver.

I tried another question, seeing as talking was not happening.

Where are we going?

Ash tipped his head. "Ah, that is not something I can tell you. Because despite cutting off your connection to Rufus, I cannot cut off your connection to your friends. And I am quite sure they will come looking for you. We need them, of course, but away from the House of Wonder. You are the bait."

Beside me, my uncle grunted in agreement. "They are stronger than anyone realized, especially together."

You want my crew too?

They nodded in tandem, and I managed to move my head a little to look from one to the other. Damn it, I could not let them use me as bait, but I didn't have a lot of say at the moment.

"We have company, boss!" the driver shouted,

his voice high-pitched and squealy. And a hell of a lot of afraid. Goblin was my first thought.

A bellow outside like the boom of a train horn echoed heavy through the air, reverberating in my chest. The start of a warning ran down my spine, but there was nothing I could do about it. No running away for me.

I turned my head a little to the left and got a glimpse of dark gray hide and the brilliant white of a massively curved horn only a second before we were hit broadside with the force of some serious tonnage.

The metal around us screeched, and every window imploded, sending shards of glass shooting through the air.

The SUV was sent airborne and tumbled sideways, spinning away from our attacker.

I was suddenly glad for the fact that ol' Uncle Shadowkiller had buckled my butt in, as we were far from done with the whole rolling over business.

Three times the vehicle tumbled before it finally crashed to a halt against a building, the horn stuck and blaring, other vehicles honking around us, a woman outside screaming for someone to call 9-1-1.

Upside down, hanging from my seat belt, I realized the spell Nicholas had put on me was gone. I turned quickly to see my uncle out cold, blood running from his head into his blond hair, breathing shallow.

A bellow rippled through the air again and I twisted to see another glimmer of dark gray hide lit up by streetlights and billboards. Another hit was coming, and if I didn't get out, I was going to have some serious bruises.

I wasn't getting another chance like this. Scrambling, I yanked the belt off, flopped unceremoniously onto the ceiling, turned and crawled out the window closest to me, the frame bent but still big enough for me to slide out.

"No!" Ash yelled, but I was not slowing down for him. Maybe he wasn't yelling at me, though. Maybe he was yelling at whatever hit us.

In my escape from the window, I sliced my left arm in a long gash that went from the top of my wrist almost to my elbow, but the pain barely registered. I didn't have long before my uncle would be awake—I had to move fast.

I stumbled a half step as I hit the sidewalk, taking in the people around the wreck, staring and pointing. Taking pictures. More screaming as the rolling thunder filled the air. Not from the night sky above, but from below.

What felt like an earthquake rumbled from the soles of my feet up through my calves, and the world slowed enough that I turned to see a freaking *rhino* charging the SUV. A damn rhino, loose in the middle of New York City. Only . . . it was bigger than any rhino I'd ever seen or heard of. Closer to the size of an elephant. The critter's horn had to be at least seven feet long, and a foot around at the base where it connected to the forehead.

That was what had slammed into us. And it was closing in for round two.

There was no doubt I was seeing one of the shifters from the House of Claw trying to stop the Shadowkiller.

"Cats on fire." I whispered one of Pete's sayings as time sped back up, and I dove out of the way. The muscular beast lowered its head and slammed its horn deep into the SUV, lifting the vehicle on the point in order to ram it again into the building's wall.

Above us, people in the building cried out, and the sound of breaking glass had me covering my head and springing back to my feet.

I ended up in the middle of the street, but traffic had stopped as the scene around us played out. What the hell did the humans here think of this madness? They probably assumed the impossibly proportioned rhino had escaped from a zoo. Did New York even have a zoo?

More important than the zoo situation . . . did I stay to make sure the Shadowkiller was done?

No, I wasn't that stupid. I knew when I was outgunned.

Did I go back to get my friends?

Bait, they'd said I was bait to draw my friends away from the House of Wonder.

The decision was made for me.

As I turned on my heel to run, the gargoyle burst out the front windshield of the SUV, dragging someone with him. He had the Shadowkiller gripped under the arms with his powerful foot claws—saving him from the shifter. I watched as Ash flew past me, body shimmering with some sort of soft glow. The humans didn't see them, their eyes riveted on the accident scene.

But I could feel my uncle's magic curling toward me, wrapping its coils around me again as he woke up.

I had to move. I had to get away, even if I didn't

know what direction was best. I bolted, running down the middle of the street, sliding between cars, feeling the threat at my back increasing with each second as Ash circled back toward me.

"Crap, crap, crap!"

What I wouldn't have given for my dad's rifle. Or a bow and arrow. Maybe a rocket launcher since I was making ridiculous wishes. I could almost hear Wally's voice whispering my odds of knocking the gargoyle out of the sky, based on which weapon I had.

Ducking around a furniture-moving truck, I used it for cover as I slid down an alleyway to catch my breath. Back pinned against the brick wall, I stayed still, listening not only with my ears but with my body.

The cut along my left arm throbbed a little, but it was already scabbing over a bit. I checked it out, but it wasn't too deep and wouldn't require stitches at least. I flexed my left hand, the pull of the muscles on the open wound a bit bothersome but not too bad.

Slowing my breathing, I looked up at the buildings around me. They blocked out much of the light from the streets, covering me with shadow.

As far as I could tell, I'd lost Ash and my

uncle. I sucked in a breath and then took quick stock of myself. Exhausted from the spell, yes. Not sure where I was? Also, yes. I could feel my friends in the distance, and that would lead me to them.

But if I did that . . . did that mean Ash could find them through me? Worse, whatever bait I represented meant I'd play right into his hands if I let my group come to me.

"Stay away," I whispered, sending that sensation through to my friends. "I've got this."

Hell, I knew I didn't 'got this,' but if I was bait, then I had to stop them.

My guts twisted as I thought about what would happen to my friends if they came after me. I had ties to Ash, whether I wanted them or not; my friends; and on a lesser scale, my uncle.

Eyes closed, I searched for that connection between me and Ash. There, like a pale blue mist behind my eyelids. Next to it was another set of ties, golden, strong. That was my bond with my friends. And underneath both, a very thin red line. A tie of blood to my uncle.

"Okay, okay, I can do this." I loosened my shoulders and tried to shut off my connection to Ash first.

I thought about stuffing the blue mist into a gunnysack.

It worked . . . only it took all the other connections with it. I grimaced and rubbed at my face, silently wishing that Ethan were there. Only because of his understanding of magic, of course.

"Again," I whispered. I pulled out the three different threads that were bound to me, took the blue misty one and stuffed it away. Once more, they all went.

"Damn!" I snapped and whacked the flat of my hand against the building behind me.

I couldn't shut off just one connection. I had no idea how, nor did I have the luxury of time to try to figure it out.

Which meant I had to cut them all off. The one upside was that it would keep my crew from tracking me down.

I closed my eyes and focused on that feeling of my friends, pushing them away one by one into the gunnysack I could see in my head. Wally, Orin, Pete, Gregory, and even Ethan though I'd tried to cut him out of our crew, each blinking out like a lightbulb switched off. With them, I pushed the blue mist connection to Ash and the thin red line to my uncle.

Which was all well and good, only it was too late. I'd taken too long.

A whoosh of leathery wings and the sound of feet thudding on the ground spun me to face the darker end of the alley. I couldn't see the full details of the gargoyle, but his outline was clear enough.

"I told you I could find you anywhere," Ash said, "and you still ran? Why? We need you, Wild. Your uncle needs you."

There was no spell on me, nothing holding me in place. "Is he dead?"

Ash shook his head. "It will take more than a car wreck to kill Nicholas, though he is slightly injured. He waits for me to bring you back. Come."

I reached into my pocket and pulled out my knife. Not the curved one made by my uncle during his time at the academy, but the one my father had made me. The knife that had helped me survive this far.

I settled into a fighting stance. "I'm not going, and if you think you can make me, then good luck to you. You're going to need it."

His wings tucked in close to his body. "Ah, young one, you are full of passion, just like your mother was. But passion can lead you astray, and we are running out of time." He snapped his fingers at me.

That same blue mist I'd seen inside my head? Yeah, it curled out from his hands and went straight down, disappearing into the cement.

"That's all you got?" I said.

The ground below my feet hollowed out, and I yelped as I fell through concrete, through layers of dirt, down until I hit the hard bottom of something, knocking the wind out of me.

I rolled to my belly as I fought to breathe and my eyes adjusted to the semi-darkness. A deep tunnel stretched out in front of me. My ears picked up the faint creaking sounds of electricity trying to click on, the buzz and snap somewhere to the right of me. Where the hell was I?

Ash dropped down beside me, landing on the wrist of the hand holding my knife, sending a blinding song of pain up my arm. He bent and scooped the blade up.

"Your father made this? Interesting, I wouldn't have thought he'd be capable of such a weapon." He tucked it into a leather backpack, then slid the strap over one shoulder.

I swung a leg out and kicked him in the back of the knee, sending him sideways and off my wrist.

Move, move, I couldn't stop. I had to get away from him. Even if it meant leaving my knife behind.

Up and running, I bolted deeper into the tunnel. Maybe it was the wrong way, but right then, it didn't matter. I had to get away from Ash, from the Shadowkiller, and find a way back to my friends.

Because I had a feeling the longer my crew and I were apart, the more danger we were in.

2

WALLY

The cab driver seemed more than a bit discomfited by the fact that six people—a couple of them big guys with wide shoulders, and one seriously grumbly honey badger—had crammed themselves into his rather small car. "Pier 36, you said? That's where the bombs went off a few days ago, isn't it? You sure you want to go there?"

"Yes," I said softly, turning the key over and over in my fingers. It had been in Wild's possession, but she'd dropped it when the Shadowkiller took her. Right after Colt died.

The flag of the key was intricate, and I ran my thumb over it. Colt's death had hit the boys hard. Ethan especially, by the way his grief and horror were barely contained. I . . . well, I had a different view of death. Colt being gone was sad, but death wasn't the end in my world. Not by a long shot.

I was in the front seat, the four boys crammed in the back. Pete was curled up at my feet in his honey badger form. As we drove, he let out little snarls here and there. I reached down and put a hand on his back. "We'll find her, Pete. Just don't . . . you know." Shift. Shifting would be bad right now.

He grumped and curled up, his nose tucked close to his body. If I concentrated, I could feel his irritation through whatever bonds tied us to Wild.

Something had changed in those moments before we left the House of Wonder. It was as if the danger we were in had ramped up our abilities and our connection to one another. More than ever, I could feel my friends, their emotions, and I suspected I could find them if we weren't together.

Maybe the same was true for us and Wild?

I closed my eyes and focused on her, to see if I could pick up a direction maybe, but there was nothing but static rolling back to me. No, that wasn't entirely true. Nothing but the many, many dead of New York City clamoring for my attention.

Outside the window of the cab, they floated

here and there, most not even realizing they were dead. Men, women, children from all races and all walks of life. Worse were the ones who saw me and understood I could see them.

If I focused on them individually, I could see how they had died. Plague. Lynching. Arrow. Knife. Trampled. Smallpox. There were no ghosts from people who'd died of old age, not here in the heart of the city. Not here where death ruled. There were so many, I couldn't even begin to calculate the numbers. Percentages were off the charts.

"You sure? Kind of a mess out there," the cabbie said, bringing my attention back to him. "Lots of cops sniffing around. Kids like you could get in trouble just for being there."

"How much farther?" I asked, ignoring his suggestion.

"Oh, another thirty minutes at least, depending on traffic," he said.

I turned back to the window, a small dead child waving brightly to me despite the grievous wounds to his face—open sores from smallpox, no doubt.

There was no way our group was going to discuss anything in front of this cabbie, and my brain was on fire as I considered all the possibilities. As Wild being taken settled into a series of numbers and percentages.

The Shadowkiller had never left a survivor before.

Her chances against a person with his power and experience were zero. Zero. But he'd wanted her for something, so maybe we had time to find her.

My jaw tightened along with my throat. I couldn't think like that. I just had to believe in her.

Now her only hope was that we could find whatever it was that this key was attached to, and that it would save her.

So, first the item, and then we would work to find Wild. That was the plan as I saw it.

A hand touched my shoulder, and Ethan spoke quietly into my ear. "I've put a spell on the cabbie. He can't hear anything."

I spun around in my seat and stared at the faces of my friends. Ethan was almost as pale as Orin and Gregory. Rory's sun-bronzed skin stood out amongst the four of them.

"Why are we not looking for Wild?" Ethan growled. "She's in danger, and we're driving around headed to the House of Shade—"

"The Shadowkiller just walked away with her,"

Orin pointed out. "We aren't strong enough to stop him, not even with others helping us. We have to be smarter than him. That's the only way we are going to save her. The House of Shade is where Tommy told us we'd needed to go, and he would know. That key she dropped, it's a start."

I nodded my agreement. "He's right. We have to figure out how to help her, not just rush in and get ourselves or her killed. That won't do anyone any good."

"Whatever this key unlocks," Rory pointed at the key I still held, "it has the possibility to save Wild. Tommy believed it. I believe it."

Ethan snorted. "Tommy's dead, right? So obviously it's not the godsend you think it is. And if it is, why didn't he use it to save himself?"

I blinked and Tommy appeared, perched on the center console between me and the cab driver. The cabbie shivered. "Damn, got cold in here all of a sudden. Turn up the heat, would you?"

I did as he asked but spoke to Tommy. "Is that true? What Ethan said?"

"I never found what the key fit," Tommy said. "I was looking for something when I was called to the House of Wonder. I remember that much. But I always thought that the key went into something in the House of Shade."

"The House of Wonder. Where you died," I said.

The others were looking at me, waiting. I relayed what Tommy had said about not being able to find the lock that went with the key.

"Does he know what it even is?" Rory asked. "A box? A door? Something else?"

I looked to Tommy, who frowned and shook his head.

"I think my mother told me the key would lead me to something that would protect me if I had it on me, something that would help my dad?" He shook his head. "That's all I remember. No, wait! She said she left it in the House of Shade when she ran from her brother. He was chasing her. She went back and got it later so she could give it to me."

I frowned and once more relayed the info, knowing that it was scattered as was so often the case with a ghost.

Orin spoke slowly. "There are stories about legendary weapons. It's possible it could be one of them. Flails. Katana blades. Spears."

Gregory was already shaking his head. "I doubt

it. All those legendary weapons are hoarded by the houses that made them. And despite the House of Shade's proficiency in wielding weapons, they don't tend to make them. They aren't much into creating things, just killing."

Rory gripped the back of the cabbie's seat. "Okay, so let's break it down. Something that could keep Tommy or Wild safe. What the hell could it be if not a weapon?"

"A spell?" Ethan offered.

"But a Shade wouldn't have access to a spell like that," Gregory pointed out. "So your theory is shit. Rather like how you treat your friends."

I closed my eyes. *Here we go again*. Gregory would never trust Ethan. And vice versa. The bad blood between the two houses was too deep, too full of history.

Ethan stiffened and then leveled a glare at Gregory. "You don't even have a clue what my life is, what I face daily. What I've survived."

Gregory shook his head as he leaned over Orin so he was encroaching on Ethan's space. "Oh yeah, I feel terribly for the poor baby born with a golden spoon up his—"

I snapped my fingers between them. "Stop. Our chances of bringing Wild back safely are slim enough. Fighting amongst ourselves is only going to make things worse."

They looked at me like I'd sprouted another head. "What?"

"What are her chances, Wally?" Orin asked. "Against the Shadowkiller."

Did I tell them that she was as good as dead before the night was done if we didn't find her? I shook my head slowly. "No. I just . . . the odds are bad." I stumbled over my words, my voice not lowering into the Walter Cronkite mimic that had gotten me my nickname. "Really bad, okay? I don't even want to say it out loud."

Zero wasn't a chance.

Silence reigned over the small interior for the remainder of the ride. I didn't have to tell them, they knew.

We all knew.

I could *feel* the fear rolling off them, as close to them as I was. Not fear for themselves, but for Wild. She was friend to Orin and Gregory. Family to me and Pete. And to the other two? Straight up love. I blinked and looked from Ethan to Rory.

They both loved her. I glared at Rory because I'd felt what had happened just before the attack. He'd broken Wild's heart somehow.

Something to do with another girl was what it felt like to me—okay, it wasn't that specific, but it had been a betrayal, and there was very little else that could have left Wild's heart that torn.

"Pier 36, or what's left of it," the cabbie said as he pulled over to the side of the road, once more disturbing my thought process.

"Pay him." Gregory reached over and poked at Ethan. "It's about all you're good for."

"Assuming I have anything on me—hey!" Ethan barked as Orin grabbed him, cringing away from the not-dead-yet vampire. Ethan's disgust and fear flared between us all and Orin's face tightened.

Yeah, we needed to figure out this connection, and how to soften it or something.

Whatever had happened had certainly changed how we could sense one another in a big way.

Gregory pulled a wad of bills out of Ethan's back pocket, throwing a glare at Ethan for good measure.

The cabbie shook his head but took the money, and we all scrambled out to stare at the destruction that was spread out over the space that had once been the House of Shade.

Chunks of cement, burned timbers and a lingering smell of smoke were the first things I noticed. A few support pillars still stood though they were partially crumbled and completely black. The footprint of the building was easily two hundred feet long and I couldn't see how deep it had stretched back.

I'd seen the House of Shade once before, and while not pretty like the House of Wonder, it had been impressive. Strong and seemingly impenetrable. All of it gone now. I blinked and a few ghosts wandered out of the rubble, kids our age.

Shades in training. Most of them didn't even look toward me. That was common with new ghosts, they were usually confused. I didn't try to make contact with them. At this stage in their afterlife they would struggle to give me information without a stronger necromancer.

Ethan dusted himself off and stood a little to one side.

"Jerks," he muttered.

Gregory made a rude motion with his hand, and I turned away from them. Whether any of us liked it or not, Ethan was one of us again. Whatever Wild had done to kick him out of our crew had reversed itself when she got taken by the

Shadowkiller. Hopefully it didn't turn out to be a mistake. Hopefully this time, he wouldn't turn his back on the crew when we needed him the most.

"There," Rory pointed to a black blasted area on the pier, pierced with a hole that went down to the water below, oblivious to the interplay of emotions between the rest of us. "That was the main building. We should start there and then spread outward with the search for . . . ." He trailed off and I knew exactly why.

Searching for something that had a keyhole, but not knowing what that keyhole might be attached to was more than a little daunting in the middle of what looked like ground zero. But we had to start somewhere.

The main building that was no more was as good a place as any. I took a step, then another and another. Yellow police tape fluttered in the air, but despite what the cab driver had said, there were no police here. Or at least none of the human kind.

Someone I was absolutely certain was a Shade stepped out of the shadows of a freestanding wall that hadn't collapsed. Right behind him was what could only be a wolf shifter. I'd seen them before, their jawlines and noses giving them away, as well as the slightly tipped tops of their ears.

"What the hell are you doing here, Rory?" The Shade was lean like a whip but moved like all the other Shades I'd ever met—predatory and smooth like he was ready to pounce on someone and snap their neck.

Rory stepped in front of the rest of us. "Barret. There was an attack on the House of Wonder. Explosions, major destruction, and the Shadowkiller showed up along with Ruby. The house heads sent kids out in groups to various places over New York in an attempt to keep them safe and out of harm's way. I'm with this group to keep an eye on them. Per Director Rufus's request."

The two older Shades exchanged a look, and the wolf shifter let out a snarl and glanced down at Pete, still trundling along in his honey badger form. The shifter's bushy eyebrows raised. "Honey badger, huh? Badass."

Pete gave a little grumbling snarl, but his pleasure was apparent through our new connection.

"You six stay here," the wolf shifter said. "We'll head out and see if we can help back at the House of Wonder."

They'd only taken a few steps when I stopped them.

"Wait, do you have any extra clothes?" I

motioned at Pete. "We left before we could grab any for him."

The shifter grunted and retrieved a small gym bag from behind a pile of rubble, throwing it at me as he and the Shade took off, heading toward SoHo and the House of Wonder. "Might be a bit big, but it'll keep him from swinging in the wind."

The guys all laughed.

When I turned back, they were gone, leaving us on the pier with nothing but the sounds of the water, and the occasional blast of a horn out on the water. A more distant rumble of traffic.

"I'm surprised they left us so easily," Gregory said. "Or that they were working together at all. That's new."

"I'm not," Ethan said, his tone sharp. "They don't give a shit about kids from other houses, and Rory is practically out of the program. Their job here was to keep an eye out for the Shadowkiller, and now that he's been spotted elsewhere—"

"That's where they'll go," Rory said. "And Gregory, you're right. It is new. Rufus is trying to encourage the other houses to work together wherever possible. But being that he's only a director for the House of Shade, his voice doesn't hold much weight."

I handed the gym bag down to Pete, who scuttled off with it behind the relative shelter of the half-fallen wall. A few minutes later, he hopped out on one foot, putting on a pair of runners that were not his own. "Not a bad fit," he said. He'd had to roll up the pant legs and the shirt sleeves, but the shoes looked good.

I started forward, then paused, uncertainty rolling through me. I held the key in my palm and Ethan looked over my shoulder.

"You know that has a spell on it, right?"

I blinked up at him. "It does?"

He took the key and rolled it over in his hand. "I mean, it's a brutally strong spell, woven into the fibers of the key itself, so if you aren't careful you could actually destroy the key."

Ethan moved to hand it back to me, but I pushed his hand away. "You have to take the spell off it, Ethan."

He shook his head. "I can't."

"You have to!"

"But I'm not strong enough! I don't know that even my father or Daniella could do it." He again tried to give it back to me, but I held up my hands. His fingers clenched around it. "I'm not trying to not help. You can't see it but there are weaves around it, like . . . a thorn bush."

I frowned and leaned over his hand, and on instinct I put my hand under his. The second my skin touched his I could see the magic he was talking about. "I see it now."

Orin and Pete joined us, each putting a hand on Ethan. "Holy cats on fire, look at that!" Pete said. "Look, it looks like the tail end of it is there."

Gregory came over to us, reluctantly. He didn't touch Ethan, but he put a hand on my arm. "So looking at it, it's a matter of unweaving the spell, not breaking it."

Ethan shot him a quick glance. "Apparently."

"So unweave it. Go slow. You have four extra pairs of eyes watching."

Rory was the last to join us, and as he brushed up against me a zing shot through to the rest of the group. "There, that black tail piece, start with it," he said.

It was not lost on me that Rory shouldn't have been able to see the magic—he wasn't part of our crew. And yet here he was, doing the impossible.

The other guys just watched Ethan, but it was Rory who spoke up. "You said you didn't want to let her down, so don't."

Ouch. But the verbal push did the trick.

Ethan's hand closed over the key and he pulled his wand from its pouch. "I'll go slow."

And slow he went. He flicked the tip of his wand against the key until it stuck to the tail end of the magic, catching it. Sweat already slipped down the sides of his face. Of course he was sick, how could I have forgotten that?

"Ethan, maybe—"

"Too late," he growled. "I can't stop now or it will break the key into pieces." He rolled the wand almost like he was winding spaghetti.

"There," Orin pointed, "under that piece."

Ethan slid his wand through a loop of magic and hissed as it touched his fingers, and through the connection I felt a flare of pain. But he didn't let go.

He kept working through the spell. Gregory pointed out a dead end and Ethan avoided it, sliding his wand around another loop that could barely be seen.

"Like a magic maze," Rory said. "There's the end of it."

"But not yet," Ethan said, a low tremor working through his body. I lifted my hand a little more, pressing my palm against the back of his hand.

"You got this, Ethan."

He didn't look at me as he worked through the last loop of the spell and the key appeared. Ethan slumped, going to his knees. "Holy shit."

Rory caught the key and turned it over in his palm. "It's different than before. It never looked like this to me."

I wondered what Wild had seen when she'd looked at the key. Had she seen through the spells? I had a feeling that was exactly the case. The key had been meant for her or Tommy, no one else.

"Rory, what does the key look like?"

He held it out to me and the second I flipped it over, I gasped.

"It's a death key," I said, marveling at the detail in the skull. "Do you know what that means?"

Everyone shook their heads, including Orin. But, of course, this was nothing any of them would understand. "Only necromancers are privy to this information, and even then, it's only necromancers who've passed a certain number of tests. But it was wrapped in a spell from the House of Wonder."

"Then how do you know?" Ethan asked from his spot on the ground. "Seeing as you've been very clear about how little your family thinks of you."

I glanced at him. "I've never said that to you."

He shrugged. "Everyone knows." He obviously wasn't in the least bothered by telling me that I was the center of gossip.

That wasn't true. Not at all. I pointed the key at him. "I know about this key because my father has a similar key. Yes, it unlocks a safe, but the safe is wound up in spells that only a necromancer could open. Which makes no sense. Why give a key like this to a Shade?"

Only . . . maybe it did make sense. I clutched the key, feeling the connection between it and Wild. No, that wasn't quite right. I closed my eyes and pinned the key between my palms. Between me and Wild's . . . bloodline?

"What is it?" Pete asked. "You've thought of something."

I nodded. "What if . . . what if Wild's mom knew that one of her kids would be a Chameleon? More than that, what if she *knew* it would be one of her children? What was it her mom said?" I tapped the key against my hand.

"Whose mom said what?"

"What is she talking about?"

Of course, they hadn't been part of that conversation. They hadn't seen Wild's mom; only I had.

I spoke slowly, thinking out loud. "If Wild's

mom somehow knew that one of her daughters would be a Chameleon, she'd know that they'd probably have a crew. And if they had a crew, there was a decent chance a necromancer would be in it." She might have even known it was Wild from the beginning.

Tommy stepped up beside me. "Then why did she give me the key? I wasn't a Chameleon."

"Then why did she give Tommy the key?" Rory echoed the question of his dead best friend, and I smiled.

"If Tommy survived the trials, she knew he'd give it to the next person to come through."

The two friends—one dead, one alive—spoke at the same time. "Wild."

"And then if Wild hadn't needed it, then she would have passed it on to Sam." Rory nodded. "Genius. Only Lexi wasn't thinking that Tommy would die. It was just luck that I saw it on Tommy and gave it to Wild after he was gone."

I doubted that. Despite the fact that he'd hurt Wild, and he wasn't technically in her crew like us, there were ties between Wild and Rory. Ties that ran as deep as any family member. The fact that he'd been able to stand there with us and see through the magic was a testament to that.

"Don't underestimate what you mean to all of us," I said.

A pulse of energy tugged on my palm, between me and the key, stopping me from thinking on it further. I took a step, then another and another. "Guys."

They were talking behind me, trying to figure out what the key went to. And how to divvy up the sections of the broken and still-smoking rubble.

"Guys?" I called again as I was drawn toward the blasted-out building.

I didn't know what it was inside of the demolished building that called to me, not right away. My eyes closed as my feet drifted toward the rubble. A song started playing quietly, just a few notes at first, but it swelled with each step I took.

A song of hope.

My eyes pricked with tears.

"Don't," Tommy's voice whispered. "That isn't what you think it is. You need to stop. It isn't safe. She's doing this to capture you, and through you, Wild! Necromancer, you have to snap out of it!"

The song, though, the song pulled at me, promising me something more than this place should have had to offer. My heart gave a ragged thump, and I felt the pang of something more than pain. A song of death.

Little queen, watch your step. That whisper on the wind came from Death himself.

I blinked, and there was the head of the House of Night, Jasmina. "Well, well. I wondered if I would find you here, daughter of Theo."

I cringed at the use of my father's name, as if my own was of so little importance. "Director Jasmina." I didn't curtsey, but stared hard at her, the song that had called to me fading and leaving me sweating and . . . afraid. She'd tried to lull me into a coma, and if she'd kept going after she could have killed me.

A very old trick of the necromancer's trade, one I'd almost fallen for.

Where were the guys? I turned to see they'd all tumbled to the ground and took a step back, horror flooding me. She'd killed them.

"I've slowed their hearts," Jasmina said. "An easy enough task for a necromancer of my caliber." Her eyes swept over me. "Very interesting, you are far stronger than even your father knows. Why would you hide that from him?" She paused, and as she looked me over, I scrambled to take hold of the connection between me and the guys to speed up their hearts.

For a split second I didn't think I'd be able to, and then they pulsed stronger at my command.

She smiled at me. "I can see why the new Chameleon was drawn to you." She stepped out of the rubble, her long black robes swirling around her feet.

"My father would have used me," I whispered. I hadn't meant to say that, but the words had slipped out of me.

Jasmina smiled. "Well, that is the prerogative of a parent, isn't it? To use their children to further their own position in our world."

I shook my head. "No. It isn't." This was not the place to start explaining my messed-up family.

I tried to step back. Couldn't.

I turned my head so I could look over my shoulder and gasped. The boys were still on the ground. So much for me waking them. "You cannot have them." I whipped back around to stare hard at her. "What did you do?"

"You can't guess? Then you truly are not trained at all." She clicked her tongue at me. "I suppose that is to be expected. Untrained. As wildly unpredictable as the Chameleon you are tied to."

I managed to move a foot, setting myself into a fighting stance, one that Gen had shown me in our one and only training session.

The director threw back her head and laughed. "Oh, please. You aren't serious, are you? Ridiculous little girl." She snapped her fingers at me, her death magic swirling toward me. Black, it was black as the starless sky, and it crept across the ground as if it had all the time in the world.

"Why are you doing this?" I had to find a way to stop her.

"I want to know where Wild is. I want you to find her for me."

Of course, normally, I could feel Wild in the back of my head just like I could feel the emotions of the rest of our crew. Hell, I could even feel Ethan there like a bump on a log. But I couldn't find Wild. Like something was between us, a block of some sort.

Not that I would have turned her over to Jasmina. If I couldn't stop Jasmina, I had to at least slow her down. "Why do you want her? What has the House of Night got against my friend?"

Her smile spread. "Because Frost is not done

with her. Not yet. We need Wild for one more task before she dies."

Frost. She had a Shade, Ruby. A vampire, Jared (dead thanks to Wild). And now a necromancer from the House of Night. Did that mean we were looking for at least three others in her crew? They were loose, even if she wasn't, and it was clear they had every intention of busting her out.

Jasmina held her hand out to me and flexed her fingers. The deep black of her magic curled up and around my body, not unlike the snake that had crept into our room. I didn't dare take my eyes off her. "I won't help you hurt her. You can't make me."

"Ah, but you will come with me. Because if you don't, I will kill all five of those boys right now. Every. Single. One of them."

My throat tightened. I knew a checkmate when I saw it.

I wiggled my fingers into my pocket and pulled out the key. If one of the boys found it, maybe they could still save Wild.

I let it fall as the older necromancer grabbed my arm and pulled me with her. Her dark eyes swirled with power and anger. "Wild killed one of our crew. Don't you think it's only fair we do the same to her? Just one, don't you think? Yes, I do too."

Her words were strange. As if she were answering someone only she could hear. Not that it mattered.

Her hand lifted, and she held it toward the boys. I screamed as I tackled her, knowing that what I was about to do was as forbidden as bringing Ethan back to life.

"NO!"

3

WILD

The tunnels I'd been dropped into by Ash were old, far older and narrower than any of the subway tunnels currently in use. The sides were made up of old, crumbling brick that broke away in pieces under my fingertips.

But despite the obvious age of the tunnel, there were emergency lights flickering here and there, enough that I could see my way as I ran. Not that I planned on being in this place for long—the goal was to find a way out. I ran with my hand against the wall, looking for a ladder that would take me up and out of this place.

"You cannot outrun me now," Ash said, and his voice sounded sad of all things. "I can find you."

Either he hadn't checked the connection between us, or he was relying on his damn gargoyle ears to track me.

"I'm not going to just let him, or you, take me!" I shouted back.

"He is not what you think. And he needs you to trust him."

Stupid, that was a stupid request if I ever heard one.

Ash's voice echoed, and I knew he was close. Very close. My hand slid over a depression in the wall. Not an alley or anything so convenient as that, more like a hollow where the ground behind the brick had sunken, right next to a vent that had a curl of foul air rolling from it. But . . . if I could do what Rory had done for me in the forest when the Shadowkiller was stalking me, I might have a chance. Hiding was a Shade talent. If I did what he did—cloak myself in shadows and slow my heart—then maybe Ash would walk right on by and I could backtrack.

You know, do something I'd never done before and hope that I could pull it out of my ass.

I pressed my back into the depression and closed my eyes, willing my heart to slow as I breathed slowly, doing my best to ignore the stench from the vent. Thinking about how it had felt with Rory's arms around me that night, how the calm and stillness had crawled over me.

I was sure now it had been the Shadowkiller scouting the grounds, looking for an opportunity to take me even then. I breathed in and out, thinking of the shadows and willing them to hide me, to let me disappear in plain sight, even as I continued to block myself from the threads that tied me to Ash, my friends, and my uncle.

Slowly, my body felt as though it melted into the stone and cement at my back and sides as my breathing continued to slow. Calm flowed over me, and my heart slowed dramatically.

Footsteps padded still, closer and closer, long talons scratching against the stone ever so quietly.

"You cannot hide from me," he said, right in front of me, the shape of his body just visible in the dim light of the tunnel through the narrow slits of my eyes. I didn't move and kept my mind focused on one thing. The quiet safety I'd had with Rory, the feel of his body tightly pressed against mine, protecting me, his breath against my ear and the slowing of both our hearts. The way he'd whispered to me and kept the fear that had been roaring through me quiet, which kept me from bolting out right in front of the Shadowkiller.

Which only left me feeling . . . empty this time. Rory should have been with me, holding me. Instead of kissing Gen. A spurt of emotion sent my heart rate escalating and I caught it quickly, slowing it. Pretending he was with me.

My heart slowed further, the shadows around me deepened, and I sunk in more, pulling the shadows around me like a thick blanket. The vent covering my scent.

If there was ever a moment where I'd doubted I was a Shade, it was wiped out as the shadows closed around me, keeping me safe.

The footsteps moved on, down the tunnel. I waited for a solid two minutes before I couldn't stand it any longer. I took a deep breath and stepped out of the shadows. Moving quickly, I headed back the way we'd come, on the other side of the tunnel. I ran lightly on my toes, keeping my steps even and smooth, and still with a hand on the wall. There was no way that there wasn't a single ladder in here.

Sweat slid down my spine more from the effort of keeping all the mental stuff in check than the physical exertion of running. I needed an image, something that would mentally put all the bonds that were tied to me in a quiet space, apparently something better than a gunnysack.

The old metal grain silo back on the farm was impossible to get out of if you fell in. Jogging along, I put the gunnysack with the bonds to Ash, my uncle, and my friends, into that grain bin and threw the lid shut, locking it.

I blinked, and the sensation of being chased eased off. Of course, I couldn't pinpoint Ash now either, but it was the best I could do, all and all, considering.

I picked up speed, the light ahead of me shifting and flickering. A single beam from above as a flashlight flicked around the floor of the tunnel. Someone had to have reported the sinkhole.

"Hey, anyone down there? NYPD, anyone hurt? Hello?"

I had to take this chance. My gut said that if I called out, Ash would hear me, but this was my best shot to get out and I had to take it. No matter my skills, jumping straight up twenty feet wasn't one of them.

Steeling myself, I whisper-yelled. "I fell!" I called up, "You got a rope?"

A tingle of warning coursed down my spine, and I twisted around to look into the darkness. Ash was coming. I didn't have to see or hear him to know.

"Hurry!" I yelled up. "There's . . . a fire down here." God, I sounded like an idiot. "It's smoky!" I fake coughed.

"Hold tight, I got one in my trunk!" the cop yelled back.

That tingle intensified. There was no way I would make it out in time.

I turned to face the oncoming gargoyle. I had only one weapon on me—the spinning knife my uncle had made—and I didn't think it would be enough to slow the House of Unmentionables alumni.

Or would it?

I pulled the circular weapon out of my pocket and hit the ruby in the center. The four curved blades popped out, catching the bit of light from the surface above me. Turning, I faced the southern edge of the tunnel but spoke to the cop. "Please hurry."

That warning up my spine? Yup, it redoubled, making me want to dance on the spot. The adrenaline spiked inside of me, dulling every ache and pain from the day, stealing some of the exhaustion that would slow me down.

"Young Shade," Ash's voice curled out of the darkness, "you cannot run from him forever. Eventually, you will be broken by this path you are on if you do not come with me now."

"But I sure as shit on my muck boots am going to try." My eyes searched the shadows in the tunnel looking for that one glimmer of movement that would give him away. But that skin of his, pebbled and gray, was helping him hide as surely as if he were a Shade himself.

The sound of a rope slithering through the air behind me. "Can you grab it? I'll pull you up!" the cop yelled.

I reached behind me with my free hand, not looking away from the tunnel. Wrapping the rope around my wrist, I grabbed hold of it. "Pull me up!"

The rope tightened, and I was pulled a foot off the ground as Ash leaped from the shadows, clawed hands outstretched.

I kicked up and out, catching him in the jaw and spinning him away, but his wing smacked me, twisting me in the air, too. The spinning knife wasn't going to do me any good. I was better off with both hands on the rope.

I knocked the blades back and stuffed it into my pocket and grabbed the rope with both hands, climbing for all I was worth as the cop pulled me upward.

A clawed hand wrapped around my ankle. Above me, the cop grunted. “What the hell?”

“Something grabbed hold of me! I’m stuck!” I yelled up at him as I kicked at Ash. “Don’t let go!”

The gargoyle didn’t snarl, didn’t slash at me with his claws. I wondered why, a split second before the ground began to shake again. A whisper of his blue misty magic curled up to soften the ground.

He didn’t need to hurt me to make me fall from the rope.

His magic burst around us, eating away at the edges of the large hole above us. The cop yelled, and the rope swung to the side as he let it slide, lowering me. My foot touched the ground, and I spun off it, slamming a roundhouse into Ash’s chest, sending him flying backward again.

I pulled the spinning disc weapon out of my pocket once more and threw it into the darkness, flinging it for all I was worth. There was a snarl of pain and then the blade was flashing in the light as it soared back to me. My hand shot out, almost on its own, and I caught the spinning weapon. I shoved the curved edges back down, stuffed it back in my pocket, and leaped for the rope once more.

Hand over hand, I went straight up, every second thinking that I'd be grabbed from below, that I'd be tackled to the ground once more.

As I reached the top, hands helped me up the last bit and over the lip.

"Kid, you okay?" The cop crouched beside me, his eyes wide. He'd called me kid, but he wasn't much older, maybe a year or two with those baby fat cheeks of his.

I nodded and swallowed hard. "Yeah, I'm okay, a bit bruised but nothing bad." I pushed to my feet, knowing that my time was limited. I had to keep moving. I had to keep going.

But where?

"You should wait for the ambulance," the young cop said, "to check you over, make sure you didn't hit your head or anything from the fall."

I waved him off. "Thanks for your help, but I'm good. A tumble won't hurt a farm girl like me."

There was a small crowd and I pushed through it, blending with the other people while the young cop called after me. No, that wasn't true. I was covered in dirt and blood, my clothes were ragged, and a quick glimpse in a shop window revealed I was in even worse shape than I'd thought. This would not help me blend in, even in a city like the Big Apple.

If being pulled through a knothole backward in the middle of a barn fire was a real thing, I was looking at it.

I needed clean clothes, a disguise if I could find one, and another weapon, and I needed all of that fast. At least it was night, and the semi-darkness of the street helped cover some of the grunge.

But that wouldn't last, and I had no money to help me get out of here. I didn't have anything. Even my wand had been lost in the fight with my uncle. I groaned quietly as I hurried through the crowd that had gathered to see the giant hole in the ground. Down to the far end of the alley I went, then hopped a fence and found myself on a wide-open street, traffic backed up as far as the eye could see.

The crush of people might help me in the money department. Ahead of me was a group of women all dressed to the nines right down to their red heeled shoes and glittering handbags. Each one of them dripped with a few pounds of sparkling jewels and gold. Maybe they were going to a Broadway show. Maybe they were coming home from a girls' night out. Not that it mattered.

The light around us wasn't great, so it was possible I could lift something off them. I strode toward them, using other pedestrians as cover until I was close enough to hear the women chatter.

"OMG, did you see what that Kim was wearing? All that outfit did was show off how big her ass really is."

A round of giggling followed the woman's words, and I took that moment to slide beside the woman on the outside edge of the group, dip my hand in her purse, and quickly lift her wallet.

Tucking it under my shirt, I hung a right and ducked down another alley, waiting to hear someone shout that they'd been robbed, but there was nothing.

There wasn't even a flutter of wings from Ash. For the moment, I'd thrown him off my tracks. I hoped. Sweat broke out along the back of my neck again, but there was no warning lighting up my spine for once.

A few people shot me looks, and I didn't blame them. I made homelessness look like a goal.

"Hey, kid."

I turned to see a tall black man with a thick mustache and no hair standing at the mouth of the alley. I hunched a little, ducking my face so he couldn't see me clearly.

"What?"

"Easy, kid. You got a place to stay? There's a youth shelter not far from here." He gave me a smile as I peered up at him from under the edge of my ball cap. "Good place to get a shower. Maybe some clean clothes. A good meal and an even better night's sleep."

I wanted to say no. That I was good on my own, but I could feel a different truth in my bones. I needed help. I needed a minute or two to breathe. "Thanks. Where is it?"

He gave me directions, and I gave him a quick nod of thanks.

"Take care, kid. Tomorrow will look better. I'd lay money on it. And if you go the the shelter, tell them Carson sent you," he called after me as I hurried off the way he'd sent me. There was no tingle of warning. No one was after me at that moment, but I still felt the weight of threats at my back.

I turned around as he disappeared. I don't mean around a corner.

I mean he damn well disappeared. Into thin air.

"Well, shit." Was he a ghost? Or something else? My money was on something else.

I ground my teeth, hating the indecision. He'd given me no reason not to trust him, but free advice from someone who was there one minute and gone the next . . .

Taking a chance, I followed his directions. And a few blocks over, I found the shelter he'd told me about. Down a set of stairs, it was underneath a block of buildings housing second-hand stores and a food bank. The sign on the door was covered in dirt which made it hard to read. I brushed my hand over it.

Castoffs and Outcasts.

I grimaced. That was not what I would call a "feel good" sign. But it was all I had, and I would take it, at least for a few minutes. A place to gather my thoughts and figure out what direction I was running.

I let myself into the shelter and took a quick look around. The matron running the place waved me over to a desk. "Come on in, don't be shy. You look like you could use a good clean-up and a place to lay your head."

I walked over to her, keeping my shoulders slumped and my head down, doing my best to keep my face covered.

She shoved a bunch of stuff into my hands. "I'm Mary. Here's a stack of towels, soap, and toiletries. You can change into these." A pair of fluffy bright pink pjs went onto the stack. "And we'll wash your clothes for you. After that, I'll give you a room. If you're hungry, we have food too."

Too easy.

I shoved the towels and bright pink pjs back at her. "Thanks, but I just need to sit a few minutes and think about my next step."

From under the brim of my hat, I could see her eyes widen. "You sure? We have room. And you'll be safe here. I promise."

False, her words felt false. "I'm sure."

She tapped a pen on the table. "Don't suppose you will give me your name? So that if you have family wondering how you are, we can let them know you're okay?"

The urge to give her my name so she could call my dad was there and then gone, an impossibility. I was dying to know how he was, to talk to him and the twins, but I had to keep my family safe and that meant keeping away from them. I shook my head again. "No, thanks."

I took a step back and pointed at an empty table. "You mind if I sit there?"

"Go right ahead, and if you change your mind, you just come on back over here." She patted the top of the towel stack and pointed at the fluffy pink pjs.

While getting clean was a priority, running through the streets in bright pink pjs wouldn't exactly help me blend in, so it was a no go.

I slumped into my seat and put my back to the wall so I could see the doorway. Just in case Ash managed to follow me.

I pulled out the wallet I'd lifted from under my shirt and laid it on my lap. The symbol on it told me it was a high-end brand, but for the life of me I couldn't think which one. Prada maybe? Burberry? On a quick count there was just over four hundred dollars in cash and a couple of credit cards. Those wouldn't help me unless I used them right away. But maybe I could use the wallet for a trade. It had to be worth a couple hundred bucks. Then again, it was clunky and no one would think for an instant a street kid owned an expensive wallet. I lowered it under the table and tucked it between my feet, hiding it from view.

Movement out of the corner of my eye had me swinging around to my left. A girl approached me, her eyebrows raised, and her mouth was turned up like she was laughing at me

Even though I looked away and angled my back toward her, she still came and sat at my table. Her gaze dropped to the wallet at my feet before lifting to me.

“You look a little lost,” she said. “Me too. That’s what this place is, made for the lost ones.”

I glanced at her. “I’m sorry, did it look like I wanted to talk?”

She grinned at me. “No, your kind usually don’t. Though to be fair, *your* kind rarely end up here. They usually die before they ever get kicked out.”

Your kind.

My heart picked up speed. “What do you mean?”

She leaned in and flashed her pointed teeth at me. “Your kind. A Shade.”

4

WILD

The not-dead-yet vampire girl sat across from me in the youth shelter. "How did a Shade end up getting kicked out of the academy? Because you don't even really need magic for your house. They'll even keep the nulls if they're good enough at killing. I mean, it's not like they're worried about you dying anyway."

I blinked a couple times and didn't bother to answer her questions because she seemed far too eager to buddy up with me. After the guy who'd given me directions here had just disappeared, running into a not-dead-yet vampire was no small coincidence in my opinion. Then again, it shortened any explanations I needed to give.

"I need weapons. I've got some cash. If you can

help me with that, we're golden. The rest is none of your business."

"You can call me Izzy," she said. "And I can get you to some weapons for sure. But is that what you really want? Are you here working for one of the Chameleons?"

I had to work to keep my jaw shut for fear it would bang on the table. "I'm not working for anyone." I shook my head. "What do you know about the Chameleons?"

"That'll cost you." She turned her hand palm up. I pulled a twenty-dollar bill out and put it into her hand. She smiled and leaned forward, beckoning me to do the same. I made myself lean close even though I could see dried blood on the corner of her mouth. "The two of them are battling it out to see who will rule our world, and they are sending agents out everywhere. We had two come through already this week. One from each."

I tried not to get excited. "Ruby one of them? Big gargoyle the other?"

Her jaw did drop. Apparently, I'd stolen her thunder. "How did you know?"

"I have my sources." I leaned back in my chair.

She blinked and leaned away. "You didn't get kicked out of the academy, did you?"

I shook my head. I didn't feel the need to tell her I hadn't graduated. Maybe would never graduate at this point. I mean, assuming I made it through the next few hours alive and all.

"What is this place really?" I asked. "It's not just a youth shelter."

She shrugged. "A waystation of sorts. You can get what you need here for a job. Maybe information on an enemy. A place to hire a hit on the competition." Another shrug and a sly look.

"Tell me about the ones who came through here." I drew the conversation back to what I needed.

Izzy tapped her fingers on the table to a tune only she could hear. "Yeah, Scar picked up some poison. The other one, he was looking for some sort of key. Said it might have gotten left behind in a bag. You look familiar, do I know you?"

Again I just shook my head. My hand went to my pocket even though I already knew my brother's key would be gone. Lost somewhere between the House of Wonder and here. Hadn't Ash ducked into and then out of the barracks for the House of Shade earlier? Could he have been looking for Tommy's key?

"Two poisons, whoever got dosed got a real

crap way to die," Izzy went on with her blabbing session. "That's what the one picked up."

I didn't bother to tell her that I'd been on the receiving end of said poisons.

"What else do you know about them?" I needed info and if I could get it from Izzy, all the better.

She licked her lips, tongue darting to the corner of her mouth.

"Well, pretty sure one of the Chameleons is still locked up. She's under heavy guard, mostly from the House of Wonder. Out on Shadowspell Island."

My guts twisted into a pile of knots. Taking into account that Ruby had broken into the House of Wonder without tripping an alarm, it didn't bode well that Frost's guards were from the same house. How many of them were working with her? Or could it be all of them?

That would be a whole pile of bull crap if it was the case.

Izzy leaned forward. "I heard . . . that the woman is going to get some kids from the academy into the prison. Going to kidnap them, like before." Her voice lowered even farther. "To feed off their energy, so she can escape." She fluttered her hands like a pair of wings flying off the table.

It could be coincidence, but I didn't think so. I had no doubt that Frost would want revenge on me for killing her vampire lover, Jared. And the best way to hurt me? Go after my family or my friends. My family was too far away for her to get her claws into easily, but my friends were right here.

Which meant both of the other Chameleons were after them.

I reached out and took her wrist in my hand, driving my thumb into the center of it. She winced and then let out a low whimper.

"When was this supposed to happen?"

Izzy bit her lip and her eyes darted rapidly around the room. "That big explosion back at the House of Wonder, you hear that?"

I nodded.

"That was when they were going to get scooped."

Her pulse didn't jump around as if she were lying. I pushed her hand away. As far as she believed, her words were truth.

I drew my hand away, narrowing my eyes at her. "How do you know all this?"

She made a motion with her hand for more

money, and I slapped another twenty into her palm. Izzy pulled out a yellow, blood-stained piece of paper. "Ruby dropped this."

The note was short and to the point.

Blow up House of Wonder. Take 2 HON, 1 HOW, 1 HOC, 1 HOU

I flipped the paper over and saw my friends' initials sketched into the paper lightly under each designation. Like a freaking recipe for carnage and how to hurt me.

Instant suspicion rolled over me. A recipe of what was going to happen landing in my hands right when I wasn't sure where to go? How dumb did Ruby think I was? How could she have known I'd be here?

Carson. The man who'd directed me here. Crap on cowboy boots, I was being funneled somewhere. Bait and push.

I stared at the note, wondering how much stock I should put into it. Just because I was being set up didn't mean that a portion of it wasn't true. "She dropped it?"

"Yeah, fluttered out of her back pocket." Izzy blinked a few times. "I waited for her to be gone before I scooped it up. I ain't stupid."

No, she wasn't stupid. But she wasn't a Shade either.

For now, I had to treat this as real. Which meant this changed everything. My friends were in serious danger. And I couldn't even connect with them because Ash or my uncle would pinpoint me.

"Damn." I pushed the paper back to her and she tucked it into a pocket.

Her smile was pasted on her face so hard, I thought I saw one eye twitch. "So. You staying here all night? Good place for a break."

"Yeah, of course." I lied right to her face and a sigh slid out of her. As if she were relieved. Not suspicious at all. "But let's get back to those weapons. I won't sleep without something sharp close by." I also needed a map to Frost's jail. "You said you know how I can get goods?"

My friends were in trouble. I was being set up. I needed to move, and move fast.

She snorted. "Yeah, yeah, you want Gordy. He's got a little of everything."

"He close by?"

"Yeah, not far. About a five-minute walk. He set up shop close by when he realized that all the losers come through here and need goods they can't get from the academy anymore." She winked. "Think of it like a black-market sort of deal."

I nodded and started to stand, but she grabbed my arm and tugged me back down, once more getting all conspiratorial on me.

Her voice lowered to a whisper. "You know something about that note I showed you, don't you? Tell me."

I shrugged but didn't look away from her. "What I know, I keep to myself."

"I'll give you a twenty back." She held out a single bill to me, and I smiled. She paled.

"Okay, okay, you keep your secrets then. That's what I deal in, so I had to ask." She grinned, but it was strained.

Izzy continued to tap her fingers on the table. "But tell me again, why send a Shade here? I mean, what are you looking for?"

I wanted to grab her and shake her. This back and forth was her way of getting info, I understood that, but it was time-consuming. And irritating.

"Checking out the black market for Director Rufus," I lied to her easily.

She tipped her head. "Gordy is not doing anything illegal, not really. And the Sandman knows about him. Everyone does. Kind of a secret that isn't, you know?"

I leaned closer, grabbing her wrist again and doing something I didn't quite understand. It was like . . . I could see her power level and it was pretty decent. "Why is a not-dead-yet vampire here? One who is stronger than she is letting on."

"Oh, that's easy, and I'll even tell you for free." She smiled, flashing her teeth again. "I didn't pass the Culling Trials four years ago. I was with a good group, it was going well, and then, well, it didn't go so well. I was left behind on one of the tests. That's all it takes, you know? When someone doesn't want you to succeed." Her smile didn't fade, but her eyes darkened and tightened at the edges. Her words and her obvious pleasure at not completing the test were at odds.

"You threw it?" She tossed her chance to get educated? Why would someone do that? Even I who hadn't wanted to be there in the first place could see the draw.

"Worked in my favor, didn't it? I'd have been in the House of Night when it went BOOM." She flicked her fingers out in a poor imitation of what had happened to the kids.

Four years ago. The same year that Rory had

gone through the Culling Trials. I couldn't help myself. "You know Rory?"

"The Shade? He wasn't in my group, but there was lots of chatter about him. One of the best, I heard. Great ass. Wish I could bite it if it still looks that good. Probably does."

I shook off the questions I had about Rory, because none were truly important. He'd made his choice in Gen, and I had to keep moving no matter that I felt a sharp ache in my chest. Heartburn, it was just heartburn. I grimaced and pushed my stupid emotions to the back of my head. I didn't have the luxury of hurting over what Rory had done. Not right then. I had to find my friends and they needed me to bring my A game.

"Okay, weapons, and maybe a change of clothes if you can get them." A map if this Gordy had one, and maybe some more info. Maybe something about just how the two Chameleons planned on taking over all five houses. Not that it would be hard now with the houses scattered and broken.

I mean, if I were making wishes, it was right up there with the rocket launcher.

Izzy stood. "Sure, come on."

She walked to the back of the room, then gave Mary a wave. Mary lifted a *wand* and flicked it at the wall in front of Izzy. Damn, I'd missed that about her. Was it because her ability was so low?

"How did she get a wand if she's a null?"

Izzy paused. "Not a null but close. Lots of nulls aren't really nulls, they're just low on the pole, if you know what I mean. And she got her wand from Gordy. Bought it, of course." Izzy went on with her explanation.

"This is where the outcasts come. You know, hence the name," she said, leading the way. "Lots move on, but some stay to help the others who get sent out into the world on their own. Like I said, that's why Gordy set up close. Lots of suckers." She laughed. "Not you, of course."

"Of course," I drawled.

Her deep red hair took on an unearthly glow as we stepped through the wall and headed down a steep flight of stairs. The soft warning along my spine didn't do more than remind me that I was following an unknown vampire. She was dangerous, but I didn't think she meant me any harm at the moment. And I was pretty sure I could take her if push came to shove.

The stairs had to go down at least two floors before they stopped, and we stepped out into a narrow tunnel. "This leads to Gordy's room. How much money you got on you?"

"Probably not enough," I said. "But I'll take what I can get with it."

"Eh, he's pretty good, especially if he likes you." Then she snickered. "But he rarely likes anyone who isn't in Unmentionables. He won't even let me stay in the room while you negotiate. Hates vamps. But I get a finder's fee, you know, for every person I bring to him."

Interesting.

The lights lining the tunnel were dim but not flickering. I had a moment where I could almost sense my crew, and I clamped down on the sensation, stuffing them all back into that silo bin I'd envisioned in my head.

I'd lay money that if Frost had them, that if that note was right, then she could somehow find me through them. I couldn't let them be used like that. But I would find them. I would get them out of danger if it was the last thing I did.

Assuming that it wasn't all an elaborate setup.

Frost would pay dearly for taking my friends.

Did I need help to make that happen? Absolutely.

I just didn't know where that help was going to

come from, and I didn't know who would be dogging their footsteps to find me. The Sandman came to mind, but he was surrounded by the other directors. People would suspect I'd go to him. The Shadowkiller would know it for sure. And Frost's people too. Probably ol' Sunshine as well knew that I'd try to get help from him. Though him, at least, I could probably trust.

Izzy stopped at the end of the tunnel and pushed open another door. "Here we go. Weapons galore."

I followed her into the brightly lit room, my eyes taking a moment to adjust.

"What have we here?" A voice I didn't know pulled my eyes to the right. A tiny goblin, smaller even than Gregory, perched on the counter. Big floppy ears dangled down over his shoulders and a super fat nose dominated his face. He had a bandage on his forehead that had bled through. "You got a need for some good stuff, eh, Shade?"

I really hoped he only meant weapons. "I do. What have you got?"

He pointed at Izzy and pointed at the door. "Out, you."

She slid back out and shut the door behind her. Gordy turned to me.

"Blades, guns, throwing knives, axes, and spears. What do you want?"

I wanted the knife my dad had made, that was what I wanted. "Knives to start." A gun would be great, but unless I got a silencer too, I'd be drawing too much unwanted attention and I doubted I could afford both. "Maybe a map. Some clothes that aren't pink or ripped."

He pointed to the shelf to his right and snapped his fingers, and a blur like mist rolled out from him, undoing a hidden latch in the shelf, reminding me of Ash's power. Only Gordy's was more of an orange mist. The secret compartment fell forward with a clatter, and blades of all styles and sizes lay in front of me.

Steel, copper, obsidian blades, a few crystal ones.

Despite the fact that Ash was with the Shadowkiller, he had taught me an important lesson in the one class I'd had with him at the academy. Weapons had a feel, and I knew what would work for me and what wouldn't. What would help me be a better fighter.

I let my fingers drift over the different handles, not even really looking at the blades until my palm warmed over one of them. I looked at where the heat had come from. A pair of foot-long daggers with bone handles and a swooping curve to each blade. Flipping them over, I stared at the mark at the base of the handle. The initials TJ. As in Thomas Johnson? My dad's name.

My heart started to beat harder. *Were* those my dad's initials? He'd made the knife that Ash had taken from me, so I knew he could make weapons. I fought to keep my voice easy. "How much for the pair of simple knives? I don't got a lot of money for much fancier."

"Both? They weren't made by anyone famous or nothing. Just a pair a null handed in years ago before he left town. I'd take . . . fifty for them." The goblin worked his way over to me. "You sure you want them? Probably better stuff here, if you can afford it."

"Maybe not, if they're cheap steel." I stepped away although it was difficult, and forced myself to look at a few other things. A bag. Some rope. A couple smoke bombs. A new shirt and pair of army pants, a black leather jacket with the letters RA stitched into the back of it.

I piled up a few other small items that could come in handy—a flashlight, a stack of bandages and a roll of gauze, a pair of beat-up binoculars, an extra T-shirt and sweat pants for Pete—Lord only knew how many times that guy ripped through his clothes shifting. There was even a stack of snacks. Still thinking of Pete, I grabbed a couple Snickers bars. Just in case. "Look, how much for all this?"

"Two fifty." The goblin made a face and rubbed at his chin. "But you still ain't got a weapon. Isn't that what you came for?"

I shrugged. How much would a map of the prison cost? Information was always more expensive in my experience than any weapon. I had to play this smart. "I have a blade. I just don't like it."

His eyebrows went up. "Maybe a trade?"

I grimaced. "Not today. I'll give you two fifty if you throw in those two daggers I looked at earlier, plus the sheaths that go with them. I won't feel bad if I break them on someone's head then."

The goblin twisted around and looked over the stuff, his mouth moving as he recounted. "Two seventy-five."

I couldn't tip my hand about how badly I needed the map. Dad had always said to walk away near the end of a deal on buying livestock and you'd see where you stood with the seller.

I pushed the stuff back and turned to leave. "I'll

get it from someone else then. Heard there's a new shop opening up."

"Wait!" He grabbed my arm, and I leveled my gaze on him. He let me go. "Wait. If you give me your word that you'll tell a few more Shades about my shop, I'll let you have it all for two sixty. Fair?"

I made him sweat while I stared at him, then finally nodded. "Fair." We shook and I took the clothes. "You got a place I can change?"

* * *

A few minutes later I was wearing a fresh shirt and jacket that smelled vaguely of moth balls. I'd sold my ripped and bloodied clothes back to the goblin for ten bucks and had my two new daggers strapped to my hips. I still had about a hundred bucks.

I circled around the room in my new clothes, looking over the remaining items. A crowbar would be handy for breaking into a jail, but too big so I left it behind. A backpack would be handy too. I put it on the counter and Gordy didn't say a word.

What else would be needed? It was hard to say without knowing what I was truly up against.

I deliberately didn't ask Gordy about the map,

leaving that for the very end to create the illusion it didn't matter. "How much?" I asked of the new items.

"Forty." He squinted up at me. "What kinda map you looking for?" He sat with his feet dangling off the edge of the table. "You mentioned that earlier."

"Hmm." I nodded. "I don't know, depends on the cost." I wasn't going to need the cash after this. I'd either get my friends out of Frost's hands, or I wouldn't. Either way . . . either way, the money was better used now.

Gordy grinned, showing flat, wide, and surprisingly white teeth. "Well, lucky for you, I make copies of all my maps. So they aren't expensive. Ten bucks each."

All that haggling earlier for nothing. I snorted. "You got a copy machine back there?" I leaned to the side to look past him into the darkness of the back room.

He laughed. "Yup. Good brand too. Even does color. So what do you need, young Shade? I kinda like you. You remind me of someone."

I gave him a tight smile. "The jail. Shadowspell Island."

His ears flapped and he let out a low whistle.

"You aren't trying to break the Chameleon out, are you?"

I shook my head. "I put her there. And . . ." Did I trust him? Not really, but I didn't think it would hurt, "she's taken some of my friends."

He jumped to his feet, ears fluttering as if he'd fly away. "Shut the front door and slap me on the ass. You're kidding me? You're *that* Shade? We heard you killed her vamp lover, that true?"

My jaw ticked. I didn't like thinking about killing Jared, because it reminded me of how his dead blood had felt on my hands, how his head lolled and showed the white of his spine. My first kill, and it had been an ugly one at that. "Yeah. That's me."

"Girly, you can have the map." Gordy jumped off and dug around under the counter, paper flying in every direction. "In fact, for that, I'm going to give you something else too. On the house, of course." The way he said *house* made me think he wasn't just referring to his shop, but the House of Unmentionables.

"Why?"

He peeked over the edge, eyes wide. "Because we can't have her finding what she's looking for, can't have *either* of them finding what they're looking for. And you never know just who is working for who anymore. Me? I work for me and my house, that's it." The little goblin stood and thrust two papers at me. One was obviously a copy, but the other was rolled and tied off with a thin piece of leather.

"This first one is the map you want. Not complete, nobody ever got a complete look in that jail and came out to tell the tale, but it's close. The other . . . the other you should read before you face down Frost or the Shadowkiller. So you know what you're really up against. And what it is that's being fought over." He touched the side of his nose and then pointed the same finger at me. "Once you read it, burn it."

The door creaked open and Izzy was suddenly at my side. Gordy glared at her. "Out with you! You aren't part of this, you lazy bloodsucker!"

She obviously had been listening to our conversation and tried to snatch the rolled parchment from me, but I caught her wrist and twisted it behind her back, dropping her to her knees.

Gordy let out another low whistle. "Been a long time since I saw anyone outmaneuver a vamp. Not since the Sandman came along."

I let her go with a push. "Not even Ruby?"

"Ruby cheats. She pulls on her connection to her master to make her faster." Gordy shrugged. "Be careful out there. If you're hunting Chameleons, remember one thing." He paused for what I could only imagine was dramatic effect.

"Yes?"

"They aren't sane. Not a one of them."

A DISGRUNTLED IZZY LED ME OUT A DIFFERENT WAY than I'd come in, while I tried not to think about what Gordy had said at the end of our conversation. Not a single Chameleon was sane. Did that mean I was bonkers too? Or would I lose my mind over time?

Another set of stairs led to a ladder, which led to a trap door that opened up into the floor of a spa, of all places. A few of the women glanced at me all decked out in a leather coat and dark jeans, but otherwise didn't so much as give me more than a quick look. Apparently, they were used to people coming and going through their spa.

"You come back if you need more stuff or more secrets," Izzy called up to me as I closed the lid over the ladder.

As soon as the lid was shut, I shook my head. "Not going to happen."

Working my way past the pedicure chairs and massage stations, I let myself out the back of the spa and into an alley.

I had new weapons, I had some gear, and even a map. And was apparently crazy or going to be. But I couldn't focus on that any more than I could on my heartbreak over Rory and my grief for Colt. My friends needed me. And I had to be on my toes for whatever games Ruby and Frost were playing.

A wave of fatigue rolled over me, and I leaned heavily against the building closest to me. I wanted to get my friends now, right now.

But if I went in tired, so exhausted I couldn't see straight, I wouldn't save them or me.

How many times had my dad told me that doing a job when you couldn't see straight was a sure way to get yourself killed? Especially on the farm. If the note was real, though, that meant my friends were being hurt. I swallowed down the fear that surged through me—not fear for me, but for them. "This is so damn shitty," I grumbled under my breath as I rubbed my face. A tic that I'd seen on my uncle more than once now. I forced my hand away from my face.

What I needed now was a place to hunker down so I could sleep for even a few hours, get some food into me, and *then* go after them.

Somewhere safe.

Where no one would look for me.

What better place to hide a dead body than where someone else had already dug up the ground to look for it? The houses had all been demolished as the Shadowkiller had searched for whatever he was looking for. No one would be there, everyone had been moved to the House of Wonder. Which one was closest, though? I went through the list in my head of where each of the houses were. Pier 36 was too far, and the Financial District was similarly situated. So it was between Central Park and the marble cemetery. Call me superstitious, but I didn't feel like it was a good sign to just wander into a cemetery at this point in my life. The last time I'd been in one I'd been plagued by zombies and almost died.

I turned my face north and headed for Central Park and the House of Claw.

5

WALLY

Tackling the necromancer Jasmina might not have been my very best idea, but I couldn't let her hurt my friends, and that was exactly what she was about to do. She screamed as we went down together, her magic blasting up into the sky like a dark beacon through the clouds. But that was not the most important part of knocking her off course, not by a long shot. We rolled across the rubble, and I tried to get on top of her again, the way Gen had shown me. Finding her wrist under her robes was tough with all that material. But necromancers weren't trained to fight, so the little bit of learning I'd done was enough to outmaneuver her.

I twisted her arm up behind her back and sat

on her while I pushed her face into the rubble. "You guys okay?" I yelled back to them while their heartbeats picked back up, one at a time. With Jasmina more worried about me, she released her hold on them.

"Cats on fire, that is hot," Pete whispered, sending a rush of pride through me.

"What are you going to do with me now, little necro?" Jasmina purred. "You can't hold me here forever."

I looked over my shoulder. "Ethan, do you have a spell that could wrap her up?"

He nodded. Though his skin was waxy and pale, he made his way over to my side. "I do."

Jasmina tried to buck me off, screeching, "Don't you dare, Helix! Your father will have your hide for this! He'll skin you alive!"

The noise was bound to attract the wrong kind of attention, and Ethan wasn't moving all that fast. I grabbed a loose chunk of rubble with my free hand and whacked it across the back of her head. "There. That should do it."

"You are amazing," Pete breathed out. "You wanna be my girlfriend?"

I blinked up at him. "What? I mean, are you

asking? I already figured the chances of you asking were less than ten percent."

Gregory gave a heavy sigh. "Maybe not right now, you two. We need to figure out—"

"She's one of Frost's crew," I said. "Infiltrated the academy. Same as Jared." Jared was the vampire that Wild had killed. The vampire who'd been Frost's lover and part of her crew.

We looked at each other, but it was Orin who spoke. "What do you want to bet each of the houses has someone tied to Frost? Jasmina here and Jared for the House of Night."

"Just like you and me for Wild," I said. "I was thinking the same thing."

Gregory patted her down, checking her pockets. "We know about Ruby. That means she must also have someone in the House of Wonder, the House of Unmentionables, and the House of Claw. I mean, assuming that's how it works? Maybe she could have more."

"Daniella," Ethan said. "It fits with how she was obsessed with Wild. She wouldn't let up about her, not once." Even as he spoke, I could feel the discomfort rolling through him. Like he didn't want to say it.

Gregory sighed. "If Professor Ash hadn't run off with the Shadowkiller, I would have said he was in on it with Frost. He's strong, stronger than anyone I've ever met in the House of Unmentionables before."

Underneath me, Jasmina stirred. I put a hand on the back of her neck, holding her down.

"Orin, can you . . . read her?"

"She's stronger than us both, she could kick us out," he pointed out.

"Try," I said. "It's all we've got."

He swept up beside me and crouched down. His hand settled over mine and his ability to bend minds rolled through me. The second his hand touched mine, a flood of thoughts burst through my mind, thoughts that were not my own.

Keys and boxes.

Frost's face as she whispered directions to Jasmina. Only fragments filtered through to me.

Spells unwoven, we need them all.

Power unlimited. For once, this world will be as it should have been from the beginning.

Death.

Bring the young one's crew to me. She will follow. That is the plan.

I gasped and yanked my hand back, sharing a quick look with Orin. He nodded. He'd seen the images too. "Frost wanted Jasmina to bring us to her. She said that where we went, Wild would follow. We were meant to be bait."

Orin crouched beside me. "We can't let that happen, Wally. There is an option."

I knew what he was asking of me—the same thing that had crossed my mind only moments before. That did not mean I wanted to do it. We were both from the House of Night, and some things were only known amongst our kind. "Orin, I know, I thought of it too but . . . that is—"

He nodded. "Forbidden, I know. But this is about survival. This is about Wild surviving, about all of us making it out of this alive." His dark eyes were hard to read. Not that he was ever easy to read. "What choice is there, Wally?"

I looked up at the sky, unable to see any stars through a whisper of cloud cover, as if I would find the answer to our predicament within the dark of the night. "There was something about key and boxes in her mind. Spells unwoven." I put a hand to my pocket where Wild's key rested. "Maybe it has to do with what got Tommy killed? With this key?"

Ethan gave a low cough and groaned. "Whatever it is you're going to decide to do, let's do it quick. I'm running out of gas while you're busy chatting away."

I turned as he went to his knees, wet coughs wracking his body. "You're this sick? You should have stayed in the House of Wonder!"

"I couldn't let her down again," he whispered, grimaced, and shook his head. "No matter what it costs."

Rory pulled Ethan up, slinging his arm across his shoulders. "Follow me. There's a place not far from here where we can hunker down, at least for the night."

I nodded. "Take Ethan and Pete, Rory. Gregory and Orin can stay with me, and we'll catch up."

"You don't even know where we're going to be," Rory pointed out.

"I can find Ethan and Pete," I said. "I can sense them." Okay, so Ethan wasn't quite as strong as Pete, and I wasn't quite ready to tell Rory that I could feel him on the edges of my mind either.

I'd leave that for Wild to tell him.

Rory gave me a quick look. "If you don't find us in thirty minutes, I'm coming back for you."

I smiled, understanding why Wild loved him—there was a fierce loyalty in him. He matched her in a lot of ways. If only he hadn't screwed it up. "Done."

He didn't ask why I couldn't sense Wild. I had a feeling I knew why—she was blocking her side of the connection to keep us safe. Maybe she didn't even realize she was doing it.

As soon as the three guys were out of sight, I motioned to Jasmina.

"Help me roll her over."

"What are you going to do?" Gregory asked as he took hold of one of the director's arms.

I bit the inside of my cheek. "The statistical probability of what I'm about to do is low, a little less than ten percent success rate."

"Except for your family," Orin said.

I drew a deep breath and slowly let it out. "Yes, except for my family."

Gregory's big eyes widened farther. "What's that success rate?"

"Ninety-nine percent," I whispered.

I put my hands on either side of Jasmina's face. Skin-to-skin contact was the most important part of this. My death magic rose up around me. My eyes were only open a little, but the burgundy red color filled my vision as it wrapped around Jasmina, digging deep into her. I didn't dare tell

Orin I'd never done this before, but I had trained for it. Scratch that, I hadn't trained for it exactly, but I'd watched my father and mother practice this on other necromancers and vampires. Especially vampires. It was all about control.

This was the very reason I'd never let my father see my full strength. I didn't want to be this person.

"Bend," I whispered the word, and below me Jasmina heaved upward, mouth open in a silent scream.

"Bend," I said a little louder, and her throat tightened suddenly, lips working.

She spoke, but the voice was not her own. "You are stronger than I realized, perhaps Wild did pick the best after all. But this one will not Bend to your will. She can't. You cannot *Bend* what is owned by another Chameleon. You can only break them."

I looked up at Orin, who shook his head but said nothing. But the look in his eyes suggested that we both knew exactly who this was speaking through Jasmina.

Frost.

"Why do you want Wild? Just because she killed your boyfriend?" I didn't think the odds of that being the case were good, but I asked anyway.

"No. The minute I realized what she was, I

wanted her power. Do you know that if you take another Chameleon's power, it can keep you alive for a hundred years? Pity I couldn't catch Lexi before she died. If I'd controlled her, I would have two young ones . . . "

Lexi? Who the heck was that?

"We aren't going to let you kill her," Gregory said. "And we'll figure out how to heal the sickness you made and keep it from spreading too."

Jasmina laughed, though it sounded as if her vocal cords were tearing from the effort. "Oh, ye of little faith, look to your own house before you cry foul on another."

"What are you talking about?" Gregory shook his head and I shrugged. I had no idea either.

"Wild is already on her way to me," the voice whispered.

"No—"

"I already have someone who has given her a clue, a way to find me," Frost whispered, the jaw she spoke through cracking with the effort. "And a reason . . . she believes I have something she loves dearly."

Jasmina's mouth snapped shut, and foam bubbled out from between her lips, flowing down her neck. From my right side a shadow appeared, flowing and immaterial, his hood covering the empty eyes I knew were in there. Death bent his hand and took her, his hand sliding through her chest and pulling her soul free from her body. Her soul twisted and writhed in his hand, reaching back toward her slumped figure. Death's hooded cloak turned toward me and his voice reverberated through my skull.

Be careful, little queen, the tides are darkening. Even you are not immune to my touch.

I scrambled backward away from the body and from Death. "The chances of things getting worse are beginning to coincide with the odds of something going wrong in a dinosaur park that opens too early. We have to find Wild, now more than ever."

Gregory held out a hand and helped me to my feet. His oversized ears were drooping. "She can't possibly mean that the sickness came from the House of Unmentionables, does she? What would we have to gain by making anyone sick?"

"Killing off the House of Wonder would do, pardon the pun, wonders for your status in the world," Orin said. "Could it be that simple? Or is this just another way to divide us?"

Gregory rubbed at his ears. "I . . . I don't know."

I dusted off my clothes. "Let's go, the other three aren't that far ahead of us. We have to tell them what we found out." I could feel the pull to Ethan and Pete, and I locked on to that sensation inside my head.

Frost was setting Wild up to come to her. Which meant we had to find Wild and stop her before that happened. With our connection to her blocked, the how of that task was beyond me at the moment.

It took us twenty-five minutes to get to where the boys had stopped—a large brick building that led into a youth shelter. Castoffs and Outcasts. That was a rather uninspiring name if you asked me.

I saw Pete first as we stepped into the brightly lit main room, but there was no sign of Ethan or Rory. "Is he okay?"

A woman sat behind a rickety wooden desk on the far side of the room, her hair pulled into a messy bun on top of her head that gave her a few inches. She pushed a pair of glasses up her nose and cleared her throat. "My name is Mary—"

I held up a hand, stopping her, seeing her for what she was in the glimmer around her skin. "House of Wonder, where are my friends? The blond one in particular. Looked terrible. Does that ring a bell?" I stared hard at her and she blanched. I wondered if I was pulling off one of Wild's infamous bitch faces. My friend was rubbing off on me.

She tipped her head. "Yes, I am from the House of Wonder, though I was exiled years ago for my inability to truly use magic in a way that my house saw fit. And your friend has already left."

"Ethan's dead?" I couldn't believe it. We'd brought him back to life even, only for him to die here, in this place? Surely I would have felt him die, as we'd all felt Colt die. I reached for the connection to Ethan and he was there in the back of my head. Relief flowed through me. And then confusion,

She held a hand up, waving it back and forth. "No. I mean your other friend. The one young Rory said he was looking for. The one with the ball cap and short blond hair, she left."

My jaw hung open, killing any resting bitch face I might have had.

Wild had been here.

6

WALLY

Pete tugged on my hand, leading me away from the main room of Castoffs and Outcasts. "They gave us a room soon as we came in, soon as they saw Ethan."

Orin and Gregory fell in with us. "Wait, why aren't we all going after Wild?" I asked. "That woman said she just left. She has to be close. We could catch up to her!"

Pete put a finger to his lips and pushed open a thin, narrow door that led into an even smaller room that barely contained the four of us and a narrow bed. "Ethan is in bad shape. Rory's the one who's most likely to find her, and he's on her trail."

"Go," Ethan said. "Just leave me here."

Part of me wanted to roll my eyes, but I

suspected that was some of Wild bleeding through to me. All the studying I'd been doing in the very short time we'd been in the House of Wonder had been on Chameleons. Their temperaments leached into their closest friends and vice versa depending on how tight of a bond they had.

I had no doubt that some of my newfound confidence came from Wild, and I was grateful for it. For days since we'd been in the House of Wonder I'd been feeling less than useless, my confidence shot. Now, though, I moved with purpose. As though I actually had an idea of what I was doing.

I only hoped that the connection didn't flow both ways, and that Wild was not suffering any of my fears.

I crouched by Ethan so I could get a better look at him. His eyes were closed, face pale, and the heartbeat that bobbed in his throat was erratic. I put my fingers to his wrist.

"You aren't a healer," Ethan rasped.

"But I know when someone is dying," I said. "And you aren't."

His eyes opened. "I feel like I'm dying."

"You're definitely sick." I stood and left the

room, heading back to where the woman, Mary, sat at her desk. "Are there any healers around?"

She shook her head. "We have some antibiotics. You'd have to talk to Gordy if you want anything . . . stronger."

Stronger was what we needed. "Where?"

The female not-dead-yet vampire approached me from the side. "I can take you to him. Rory's with him right now."

I nodded. "Take me to them."

She grinned. "I'm Izzy."

"Wally," I said.

"That's a strange name. What house are you?" She tipped her head to the side like a bird, fingers drumming on the door frame.

"Night," I replied, wondering why she couldn't tell. Usually the vamps knew us right away. "Why?"

"And your friends? I see another vamp like me, a goblin, and I'm guessing the one on the bed is a mage and the last . . ."

I frowned. "Pete is House of Claw. Why?"

"Oh, I'm just a curious thing, always asking questions, picking up new stuff. I like to know who comes through here, you know? Never know when information might just save your ass."

As if her words had been prophetic, she turned

as the main door behind us blasted open in a shower of sparks that sent everyone in the room flat to their bellies, with the exception of me—I was thrown against the far wall.

I slid down, barely catching myself before I hit the ground.

I stared into the glittering dust that floated through the smoke, the shadows of robed people appearing within it as they stepped into the opening they'd created.

The House of Wonder had arrived.

"Pete, Orin, Gregory, grab Ethan. It's time to go!" I hollered.

A figure stepped out of the dust, his blond hair and perfect posture a sure stamp if ever there was one. I'd met him once before, and he'd given me a dress for helping to bring Ethan back to life. Well, probably his wife had done that.

"Mr. Helix." A part of me wanted to bow to him, but I straightened my back and forced myself to look him in the eye. "Can I help you?"

The four boys rushed out of the narrow hall, Pete and Orin holding Ethan up. His head rolled toward his father. "I'm not coming with you."

I wasn't sure if he was talking to us or his

father. Ethan drew a breath and went on. "I won't lose her. Not for you."

Mr. Helix's face tightened. "You're sick. You'll die without help."

"I have time," Ethan said. "She said so."

She being me.

Mr. Helix lifted his wand, and I flung my hand out as I called up my magic. Death magic was a funny thing—in some ways, it was stronger than any House of Wonder power, but it could be . . . finicky when not used specifically for killing.

Deep burgundy tendrils shot from my fingers and wrapped around Mr. Helix and the two figures that stepped out of the smoke to stand beside him. The twins, Dartanion and Dallin.

"Boss?" one of them said. "We gotta get at least one of them to draw the Chameleon in, that's what Daniella said." He spoke quietly, but not quite quiet enough. "What about the others?"

Mr. Helix's face tightened. "We kill them. Those were the orders, you know that."

"You sure? They're just kids," the other twin said. I could wait no longer.

"You aren't the one who owns death," I growled. "I do."

I yanked my hand backward, and the three of

them were flipped off their feet and onto the rubble left by their explosive arrival. Why in the world they couldn't just have opened the door was beyond me, but I suppose when you were at the top of the heap you liked to make an entrance.

"Go, find Rory!" I yelled at the four guys, and they dragged Ethan with them toward the far wall, which slid open revealing a dark staircase straight down.

I walked backward, keeping my eyes on the three men who were slowly getting to their feet.

"You are going up against the wrong people, necro," Helix growled. "The wrong people. Come with us, and I think you might live. You're strong enough to be useful."

My voice pitched lower as I said, "Perhaps it is you who is going against the wrong people, Helix. Perhaps it is you who should be proving yourself . . . useful."

I slammed the door in his face, then put my hand to it, infusing it with the most painful thing I could—*death's touch*. An old safeguard that I'd been taught years ago but hadn't been strong enough to use. Until now.

There was definitely something about those terrifying moments that had strengthened me—

the first time I'd let my anger out, the first time I'd not been careful with my magic.

Like a key had unlocked something in me, some amount of strength I never knew I had before. Not even when we'd brought Ethan back to life had I felt like this.

The wood of the sliding door glowed with my magic and slowly absorbed it. Anyone who tried to open the door on the other side would be shocked —the kind of shock that packed the wallop of a set of defibrillator paddles, and their heart would stop for several seconds.

It wouldn't kill them, but it would buy us time as they recovered.

I ran down the steps as the first howl of pain ripped through the air. Three hits. The door would give three hits, maybe four if we were lucky. In other words, we had to hurry.

Once I reached the bottom of the stairs, it wasn't far to a doorway that opened into a shop of sorts. A small goblin with oversized ears and a bloody bandage on his forehead sat on the counter, his eyes wide and his hands spread out to either side. Rory stood in front of him, the other four guys now ranged out behind him.

"Tell me what she bought and where she

went," Rory demanded, and by the sounds of it, this wasn't the first time he'd asked.

The goblin fanned out his spidery fingers. "Can't. That's confidential. You know that. Wouldn't want me telling the next person what you came here looking for, now, would you?"

Rory turned as I came in, his eyes tight.

"We can find her," I said. "We have Pete's nose."

Rory looked over at Ethan. "What we need is something to keep Ethan up and moving for the next twenty-four hours. After that . . . after that, he'll need a healer for sure."

I looked at Rory and then each of the others, my friends. "They want to capture one of us, and . . ."

"Kill the rest," Ethan said. "I know."

"Well, my money's on Ethan for making it through alive," Gregory drawled.

I shot him a look and he shrugged. "You can't say I'm wrong."

No, he wasn't wrong. Ethan would be taken. And we would be killed.

"Yes, that's their plan," I whispered. "They didn't think I could hear them."

Gordy tipped his head to the side, making his

bat ears flop. "Damn, you brought the heat on me this time."

Another howl came from up top. Two down, but it wouldn't be long before they were on our heels.

"Hurry," Ethan rasped. "We have to hurry."

"Something to give him a pick-me-up?" Gordy hopped across tables to the smallest of his counters. "I got something. A bit of juice, if you will." He rummaged around until he pulled out a Flintstones vitamin jar that looked about twenty years old, the label half scratched off and the plastic dingy.

He unscrewed the lid and shook the bottle, popping two green gummies out. Literal gummy bears. "Two pills as needed. Should keep you on your feet. Right until you drop dead, that is, so take care."

He gave two to Ethan, who ate them quickly, without question.

Another scream from up above. I grabbed the bottle from the goblin. "We'll take it. And a way out."

"Hey, you gotta pay for that!" he barked.

"Mr. Helix is coming down here. You tell him

it's for his son and he can pay for it," I said as I turned toward the guys.

Pete did a slow turn and sniffed at the air, then went to his hands and knees. He shuffled along until he pressed his face against the wood paneling of the far wall. He turned and tapped his nose and pointed to a hallway that led away from the door we'd entered. "She went this way. I think."

"Go," I said as the sounds of footsteps rattled down the stairs.

I pushed the guys in front of me, shoving the bottle into Rory's hands. "Go, you have to find her." I paused. "I'll slow them down."

"No fighting in my shop!" Gordy yelled. "None!"

Rory gave me a slow nod. "Catch up when you can." Then he gave me a quick hug and kissed me on the top of my head.

I could tell he knew what I did. I wouldn't be able to catch up, not at all. If Helix caught us all together, he would kill all but Ethan. Better for Ethan to get out and for me to be caught and used as bait.

But I would make them work for it.

I put my hand on the door that led into Gordy's room and wrapped it in another touch of death.

"Necromancer," Gordy said with more kindness than he should have, considering he didn't want any fighting in his shop. "You can't go up against mages. They're stronger than you. And they've got years of training."

"There is less than a three percent chance of me being able to best these mages based on their age, strength, and general knowledge, that is true." My voice deepened, and I shuddered, shaking it off. I lifted my head and stood back. "But I have to slow them down. My friend's life, all of my friends' lives, depend on it. And I won't fail them."

"Even the goblin?" He seemed surprised.

"Gregory is smart and capable, and we wouldn't have made it this far without him," I said. "I count him as one of my closest friends."

Gordy gave me a kind smile. "You're a better friend than most deserve."

The door behind me shuddered, and a bolt of fear shot through me. I swallowed hard, my confidence in my new strength wavering. "I . . . I won't let them down. You should go. Hide if you can."

Gordy sighed. "Why is it the good ones always die so young?" He hopped off his table and went to the door the boys had gone out. He waved his hand over the wood, and it smoothed into stone and mortar as if a door had never been there. I gaped at it. That was a handy trick.

A bellow of rage came from behind me, and the main door splintered. A wand poked through and I snatched it away, throwing it across the room. Gordy caught it. "Excellent. I'll count this as payment for the damage and the vitamins."

"Damn it, she took my wand!" one of the twins shrieked.

I glanced at Gordy, and he crooked a finger at me. "You want me to follow you?"

He shrugged and then grinned. "There's always more than one way out, if you dare to follow me, one from the House of Unmentionables."

There was no choice as far as I was concerned. "I trust you more than I'd ever trust a House of Wonder mage."

His smile widened as he clutched at the wand, a glimmer in his eyes. "Well, then, let us be gone."

I took a breath and dove into the darkness of his back room.

What had I gotten myself into this time?

7

WILD

I jogged at a steady pace, using up precious energy to get where I needed to go as quick as possible. Through the dark of the night heading north through New York City, straight toward Central Park. The rubble of the House of Claw would provide me with a place to curl up for a few hours, lick my wounds, read the note that Gordy had given me, and get a plan together to get my friends out of Frost's hands.

I almost opened my connection to them to see if they really were in the jail with Frost eating their energy. Nausea rolled through me at the thought of losing another of my friends. Of feeling one of them die.

For just a moment I could feel Colt's body in

my arms as I held him, staring at his closed eyes, searching for the bond between us. Finding nothing and feeling that emptiness soar once more inside of me. One minute he'd been promising to kiss me and the next he was dead.

I struggled to breathe, fatigue and heartache finally spilling out of me as I ran. Tears slid down my cheeks, hot on my skin in the cold night air. And for those moments I let them fall, let my sorrow fill me up. I didn't dash the tears away.

Colt was worth all the tears. My friends were everything to me.

Once I found them, I should send them far away so my uncle Nicholas couldn't find them and use them against me, so that Frost couldn't use them against me. And yet, we were stronger together. And if I was honest with myself, in the short time we'd been friends, they had become more than that. A second family. One that I didn't want to lose any more than I wanted to lose my dad, or the twins.

I wove through the stalled traffic that sat at a light, rolling my hip off several car hoods, and crossed to the southernmost edge of the park. Where I immediately slid to a stop.

A warning rippled through me right before I

picked up the sound of heavy feet and a smell of B.O. that was stupidly familiar. I ducked behind a big tree, pulling the shadows around me.

"You think she'd come here?"

"No." A chuckle from the other one. "She ain't that smart. She's a dumb-dumb." Yep, that voice matched the stench.

Shaw, the big-ass, fourth-year Shade who'd attacked me on our first day in the House of Wonder. I stayed where I was as they approached, sliding around the tree to keep it between me and them.

"So, what are we doing here?" the other voice asked quietly. "Just wasting time?"

"Don't know, Graham. I just do as I'm told," Shaw grumbled. "Boss man said to radio in if we found her. But I'mma kick her right in the lady balls. Kapow!"

The other one—Graham—sighed. "Shaw, you are not the sharpest tool in the shed yourself, you know that, right?"

"I'm the biggest, though. Don't that make me the best?"

They stopped on the other side of the tree, and I let myself peek around the edge to get a look at the pair. Graham was slender, tall, wore glasses, and had a wand in his hand. He tapped it against his leg. "Why did I get stuck with you?"

"You dissing me?" Shaw growled, folding his massive arms across his chest and turning his back to me. He had a walkie-talkie clipped to his belt. That could come in handy.

"Never." The sarcasm was heavy in Graham's voice, but Shaw just grunted.

"Good. Hate to smash your face and break your glasses. That's bad luck."

Graham rolled his eyes and whispered under his breath, "God save me from this stupid lug." Speaking louder, he added, "Shaw, all I'd have to do is give you a riddle. You'd be busy for the next year trying to figure it out."

If they had been two Shades, I could've taken them. But Graham had a wand, and I wasn't sure I could do it. Besides, all I really wanted was the radio; there was a good chance it would be a direct link to the Sandman. I slid around the trunk as they continued to follow the path past the tree. Pulling the shadows around me, I stepped out behind them and lifted the radio from its loop on Shaw's belt. I was prepared for him to react to the change in weight, if nothing else, but he didn't seem to notice. I mean . . . he was a fourth-year Shade. He should've felt something.

"Not true. I'm good at puzzles. Good at finding the outside edge." Shaw actually sounded proud. Of course, the fact he thought a riddle was the same as a jigsaw puzzle said it all.

Graham was right: Shaw was a big-ass lug.

I stepped behind the tree and held the radio tightly, praying it didn't squawk. I found the volume dial and turned it down, then tucked it into my pack. Waiting for the two of them to clear my line of sight, I turned east and headed out of the park. So much for resting at House of Claw.

If people were looking for me here, would they be at all the houses? Or was this just where the Sandman guessed I'd gone?

I wanted to believe the Sandman would help me, but I wasn't so sure. His methods were . . . extreme when it came to training, and he'd made no bones about disliking me right from the beginning.

I hurried down the sidewalk, crossed the street, and tucked into the doorway of a bakery with a big overhang. The smell of bread and sweets filtered out to me, making my stomach rumble. I was going to need food at some point. The Snickers in my bag were for emergencies only.

Above the city, a roll of thunder echoed over the noise of traffic and the constant flow of people. I pulled the radio out and turned the volume up.

"Shaw, answer the damn radio." The Sandman's voice came through sharply.

I pressed the button on the side and spoke slowly. "He's not here, Rufus."

Shit, was that the first time I'd used his given name?

"Wild." The relief was . . . odd along with the fact that he used my first name. "You're not with the Shadowkiller?"

"No. I got away."

A heavy pause, then, "They're hunting you, Johnson."

"Who is?"

"The House of Wonder. Mara and I are—"

"She's okay?" I blurted out.

"She survived," he said. "Barely."

I lowered the radio and let out a breath. "Thank God."

"God had nothing to do with it, unless you want to start worshipping me? I got to her in time to get her to another healer."

I stared at the radio before I pressed the button to speak. "Are you attempting to crack a joke?"

The silence hissed and then another voice came on the line. Mara. "Listen to me, the corruption goes deep, Wild. Your brother knew it. I know it. The sickness started a long time ago, but something has changed and we didn't recognize it at first. It used to only hit nulls, but now it's hitting everyone—it's mutating and picking up speed. The attacks on the houses. Frost. The Shadowkiller. I don't know how it's all connected, but it is, and each layer goes deeper than I could have ever thought."

The soft scuffle of feet had me backing farther into the shadows. I turned the volume down again. There was no warning, no whisper of danger, but why would anyone be coming this close to me?

"I smell her," a newly familiar voice said.

I stuck my head out. "Gordy?"

But better than that . . . "WILD!" Wally screeched as she threw her arms around my neck. "Oh my hell, he found you! In a city this size, the chances were less than one percent! I couldn't even bear to tell him the chances were so small! We were following the boys, who are following you . . ." She trailed off and I could see the worry in her face. They hadn't found them yet.

So where the hell were the guys?

"Of course I did," Gordy grumbled. "You can't be a goblin with a nose like this and not be able to find someone you've met before. Might not be a shifter, but I got me some good smellers on me."

Smellers, as if he had two noses. Nope, I didn't want to know.

I hugged her back, relief flowing through me that the note Izzy had shown me was a ruse. "Wally, I have never been so glad to see you." And I meant it. I wasn't sure what I would do if she'd been hurt. If any of them had been hurt. A small shudder slid through me and Wally hugged me tighter.

"Me either," she whispered, and a matching shudder rippled through her.

She was crying so hard she was shaking. I pulled her into the doorway's shelter with me. Gordy stood on the top step and gave me a little salute. "Be careful, you two, and remember, you aren't alone out there, no matter how it might seem."

He snapped his fingers and disappeared in front of my eyes. Just like Carson who'd directed me to the Castoffs and Outcasts. Carson who'd sent me to a place where a note had been waiting for me to find.

I blinked a few times, not sure I'd seen what I thought. I'd assumed the first guy was working for Frost, but Gordy was known to Izzy and the others at the shelter. And he'd helped both Wally and me.

I didn't like this, not one bit. "I really wish people would just wear signs that said who they were aligned with."

Wally cried into my shoulder, ignoring my attempt at a joke. "They're hunting us, Wild. The House of Wonder is hunting us. I don't know but I think . . . I tried to lead them away but I think they might have followed Pete and the others."

I kept an arm around her and hunkered down so we were crouching. "What are you talking about? I thought . . ." Well, it didn't matter what I thought about Frost. The bitch didn't have my friends, that was all that mattered. "Okay, so where are the guys?"

"They're safe for now. Frost tried to take me through another necromancer," she said. My jaw dropped. Wally looked away. "It didn't go well for her."

She didn't say more but I could see the struggle

on her face. “There is no such thing as cheating in the game of survival, Wally. My mom told me that once, a long time ago. And she was right. We do what we have to do to survive. There is no shame in it.”

My friend lifted her eyes. “It was ugly.”

“Death usually is.” I slid an arm across her shoulders. She let out a breath. “Helix and the twins are hunting us for Daniella. We think that she’s working for Frost. They have orders to capture just one of us. I think to draw you in, and they mean to kill the rest of us.” She wiped her face. “How are you always so confident? It’s exhausting!”

Killed. My knee-jerk reaction was anger, but this information also went against what the note had said. Which was true? “Are you sure?”

She bobbed her head. “Yes, they practically shouted it across the room. They didn’t even care that we heard.”

I opened my mouth, and she shook her head, stopping me. “But why did you think Frost had us?”

I frowned. “Izzy had a note someone had nicked off Ruby. Frost was planning on taking you five when House of Wonder was attacked. While I wasn't a hundred percent sure, I thought there was a chance you'd been taken to the jail, and . . ."

Well, shit. My stomach could not have dropped lower. We *were* being led in different directions to keep us off our game. I bowed my head and drew in a few short breaths. Knowing it was happening was only part of the issue. The other part was what to do next.

"Okay, okay, let me think."

Thinking was hard when your friends' lives were on the line. The last time I'd done something to save the people I loved, I'd cut all my hair off, dressed up like a boy, and headed straight into the Culling Trials.

Look where that had gotten me.

"What about the boys? I can find them, I think; we got separated when the House of Wonderduds showed up," Wally said.

I looked at her. "You can find them?"

She grinned. "That connection between you and us seems to have morphed. I think I could find any of them, Rory too."

I had to blink a few times. "Rory."

"Yeah, he came with us looking for you. Of course."

The idea of Rory looking for me did strange

things to my body and I had to push all the warm fuzzies away. Like right now.

I cleared my throat. "I think I know someone who might be able to pinpoint where our hunters are." I turned the radio back on to hear a muttered curse from the Sandman. I pressed the button on the side. "We have a situation."

"*Now* you think we have a situation?" he growled.

"Frost has people hunting my friends. Any chance you can slow up the ones doing the poaching?" I paused, knowing that he would know what that meant. They were in trouble, and I needed his help.

"I'll get someone on it," he said. "Tell me where you are."

"No. I can't. I'll check in later. Do what you can, Sunshine." I turned the dial down on his shouted expletives. Yup, there it was, out in the open.

Sunshine.

Wally let out a low whistle. "You really piss him off."

"It's a talent," I muttered. "But I'm serious. I'm not letting Frost or her friends hurt any more of our crew. But that means we can't play into her hands either."

"I know. I'm with you, Wild. No matter what." She smiled and then grabbed my arm as I sagged against the door behind me, exhaustion working its way through me. I'd been injured, healed, and on the run too many times in too short of a space of time.

"So we go find the boys?" Wally said.

"Where are they?" I asked again.

She closed her eyes and slowly lifted a hand and pointed east. "I'd guess about an hour that way, moving toward me but slowly. I think . . . I think that they lost your scent and they are trying to find us but . . . the connection doesn't seem to be working quite the same for them."

I didn't think I could do an hour of walking.

"We need a place for the rest of the night for all of us. And food if we can grab it on the way," I said. "See if you can reach one of them, draw them to us."

Wally looked around. "The marble cemetery isn't far. We could go there; my family has a place that we could use. It's fairly central between us and them, so they won't have far to go either."

"I just tried the House of Claw, there is a Shade and a mage named Graham on the lookout for me, and if I remember correctly the House of Night is at the marble cemetery." I stood with her and we stepped out into the lightly falling rain.

She gave a slow nod. "Sure, but there are other places near the House of Night that will work for a quiet place to rest. Places only someone from my house would know about."

A grimace crossed my face. "You mean a crypt, don't you?"

She shrugged. "It's my family's mausoleum. It's protected by heavy spells, and it will open for me. There is less than one percent chance of anyone finding us there." She shrugged. "Unless you have a better idea?"

"Nope, I do not." Though I wished I had. Because hanging out in a crypt was not my idea of a good time. Even if it was safe. Even if it was all I had for the moment.

Wally hooked an arm through mine and headed almost directly east.

And yes, I know my directions because I grew up on a farm and if you didn't learn how to find your way home when you were over in the neighbor's quarter section, Dad had to come looking for you. Nobody wanted Dad to come looking for you.

"So you can sense the guys?" I asked. "Are they okay?"

"They are, except for Ethan. He's in rough shape, but we gave him a couple of green gummy bears and hopefully that will help him perk up until we can get him to a healer," she said.

Gummy bears? Another thing I probably didn't want to know about. Or maybe I was just too tired to care as long as he was okay. For now. "Why didn't he stay in the House of Wonder?"

"Because he thinks he's in love with you, and now has to prove it to you by coming to your rescue even though you don't love him," Wally said. "He has no idea that you are one hundred percent in love with Rory."

My jaw dropped and I stumbled to a stop, my ears ringing violently. "What? What did you just say?"

Wally didn't look at me, just tightened her hold on my arm and kept dragging me along. "Ethan doesn't realize he doesn't stand a chance against Rory. Never has." She shrugged. "But he could be a good friend and help us out of this jam, so I'm not telling him what he doesn't need to know. Or what he chooses not to see."

"I'm not in love with Rory. I mean, not like that," I spluttered. Okay, so I was lying through my teeth, but the thing was he'd made his choice in

Gen. I had to let him go in that respect. Even if Wally was pretty much spot-on about my feelings. So lies it was. "He's family. That's it."

Wally pointed at the bright flashing lights of a fast-food joint. "Let's get food to take with us. We're almost there."

"I'm not in love with Rory," I said again.

"What do you want? Just burgers and fries?"

"I'm not!" I yelped, not liking the way my voice squeaked. "Wally, I'm not."

"And some bottled water, that'll be good. We both need to hydrate. You know that dehydration counts for twenty-three thousand deaths a year? Amazing, just for not drinking up a little more." She pushed open the glass door of the fast-food joint and got in line. All while completely ignoring my protests about Rory.

She ordered a stack of burgers, fries, apple pies, and bottled water. Two overloaded, greasy bags full of even greasier food later, we were back outside and on our way to the mausoleum.

"I'm not," I whispered.

"I think a purple dragon once quoted 'the lady doth protest too much, methinks.' You do know that you completely opened up—emotionally, that is—when you saw him doing something with another girl? I'm guessing on that last bit. Putting the pieces together with how she trailed after him, I would say it was Gen?" Wally tipped her head toward me. "I don't think any of us meant to feel it. More like it was this wave of heartbreaking emotion that kind of slammed into all of us at once."

Oh. Shit. "You . . . all of you felt it?"

She nodded and picked a fry out of her bag, popping it in her mouth. "Yup. I would bet Ethan and Colt felt it too. Though, Ethan might not have realized what it was exactly. He seems to be only picking up some things since he kind of stepped away from us and vice versa. Also I think he's got blinders on when it comes to you. Like he can't imagine anyone *not* wanting him. Here we are," she said brightly as she stepped off the sidewalk and onto a paved pathway that led into a graveyard.

It was fancy, with manicured grass and flowers set in front of huge tombstones and crypts. There were even a few candles lit for the souls of the lost that were impossibly still lit even in the sputtering rain. All in all, it was a perfect place for an ambush if you asked me.

To be fair, I was scoping the location, but I was

doing it on autopilot as I absorbed what Wally had just told me. That my emotions had run over, that they—every single one of my crew—knew I loved Rory. Okay, so being honest with myself for once, yes, it was true. But I hated that I'd been rejected before I'd even had a chance to say the words.

I could let him go, if he was happy with her. I could.

Also, my middle name was surely Denial, even I knew that. I wrinkled up my nose. Emotions were as messy as a kid with finger-paint, and about as predictable.

Wally led me through the graveyard without a single pause until we stood in front of a six-foot-high crypt, the etchings over the doorway nothing but symbols. I squinted at them, feeling as though I could almost understand them.

I blinked, and the symbols morphed in front of my eyes like when I'd read the Latin in the House of Wonder.

I spoke slowly, because the words were both dark and light at the same time. "Fear not death, for it comes on gentle wings to ease your sorrows."

Wally smiled at me. "See? You're a natural." She stood on her tiptoes and brushed her fingers over the symbols before stepping back. The cyphers lit up with the deep burgundy of her magic, a flash in the darkness that was there and then gone like a lightning bolt.

"That should do it," she said.

Deep burgundy? "Wait, your magic was pink before, wasn't it?"

Wally ducked her head. "When the Shadowkiller took you, I . . . things happened. My magic seemed to shift into high gear. So did Gregory's. Ethan broke a spell at the pier that he shouldn't have been able to, and Rory's slowly connecting with us. I think that fight changed things for all of us."

Before I could ask another question, the door slid open, moving on silent, well-oiled hinges. I pulled the flashlight from my pack, and in we went, checking the space over. The walls had deep, coffin-sized recesses, but none were full. The entire crypt was maybe ten feet by twelve and completely dry and empty of anything but a bit of dust that we'd stirred up.

I still didn't know what was upsetting me more: that we were going to eat dinner in a crypt, that my crew knew about my feelings for Rory, that we were being hunted by two Chameleons, or that maybe Colt had felt my love for someone else and it had caused him to be reckless. A lot of possibilities when it came to being upset.

I made myself pace out the small space, running my hands over the walls, checking for anything that could be out of place despite my fatigue.

“Colt,” I finally said as the door shut behind us. “He knew that I . . . loved . . . Rory? You think he really felt that?”

“Yeah, I would say so—” Wally turned to me with her eyes wide. “You don’t think . . . that he put himself in danger because of that?”

Yeah, that was exactly what I was thinking.

If I’d thought my grief and guilt over his death couldn’t get any worse, I’d been wrong.

Dead wrong.

8

Wally and I slid to the floor, side by side. She handed me one of the brown paper bags. "You need to eat before you do anything else. Before you can even think about Colt and all the 'what-ifs' of his death." She slid a bottle of water over to me. "I can feel the guys still; they have stopped moving, but nobody is hurt or anything."

She was right and I wasn't about to argue with her. The cheeseburgers were loaded with grease and ketchup, and nothing had ever tasted so good. I downed three and a bottle of water before I slowed.

I leaned my head against the cold wall, staring at the ceiling. The flashlight sat at our feet and made a perfect circle of light above us. I wanted to flick on the walkie-talkie, but I held back. It had only been half an hour, at most, since I spoke with the Sandman. I had to give him time to find out where Frost was—if he even could.

But the truth was it was thoughts of Colt that consumed me. That he might have died because I had apparently flashed my stupid heart to the entire crew when I myself didn't even understand my feelings.

"Could you . . . contact his ghost?" I asked as I opened an apple pie and took a bite of the still-hot flaky pastry and sweet filling.

"Colt's?" Wally gave a slow nod. "Maybe. I mean, I could try. He was killed rather than dying a natural death, so there is a forty-seven percent chance that he is a restless spirit, like Tommy. But we'd have to be back in the House of Wonder to really talk to him. I'm not strong enough to draw him away from his place of death. Only about three percent of necromancers have that ability. I doubt very much I'm one of them."

"Can you try?" I asked.

She smiled but it was wobbly. "Okay, I'll try. But don't be disappointed, okay?" I nodded and she closed her eyes, sitting cross-legged across from me, her hands on her thighs as her head tipped back.

The whisper of her magic—that gorgeous deep wine-red—flowed around her and slowly filled the room. As it slid over my arms, the hair stood on end and my muscles tightened with a sudden tension. Not fear, but anticipation.

"Colt of the House of Shade and the House of Wonder," Wally intoned in her deep voice, "come to me."

Her magic swelled, spread out around us and then just as quickly, faded. Wally shot me a look. "I'm sorry, Wild. I . . . I'm not surprised. But we can try again back at the House of Wonder."

Which would be probably never at this rate. I leaned my head back and my eyes slid shut. "Thanks, Wally, I know you tried. Wake me when the guys get here."

She shuffled around until she was next to me, lending me some of her warmth. I must have fallen asleep.

Colt sat in front of me. "You have to try again, Wild. You have to."

I jerked awake, the taste of blood in my mouth. "Wally."

"What is it?"

"Call him again." I knelt and tried to shake off the weight of sleep that wanted to tug me down.

Wally sighed. "Okay, one more time."

I nodded and took her hand. "I'll help."

Once more her magic swirled up and around us, deeper in color than the first time.

Once more she intoned his name.

But this time the magic didn't fade.

There was a tugging sensation in my belly as her power rose, and on instinct, I pushed some energy toward her. She gasped and the magic swelled again, filling the space of the crypt until I couldn't see her.

But there was someone walking out of the deep clouds of magic straight toward me.

"Colt," I whispered his name, pain snaking around my heart. There had been something between us. A different time, a different place, and things . . . well, they would have played out in a totally different direction.

His smile softened as he saw me. I didn't stand —I wasn't sure I trusted my knees to hold. He stopped in front of me. "Wild. Good job. I have to tell you what I know."

"What you know?" I grimaced.

"That I'm dead? Or that you love Rory?"

I put a hand to my face. "I'm sorry. For both. This is all my fault."

His gentle smile slid a little. "I thought Ruby was focused on the Shadowkiller. I thought . . . that I could kill her when she wasn't looking and maybe prove myself. It's a flaw I've had all my life. But I hesitated. It had nothing to do with what I'd felt from you, Wild."

My guts untwisted a little.

"Are you sure? Because I didn't even know . . . what I felt exactly. I mean, I think I do now but . . . ." God, I felt like a tool just saying it out loud.

He crouched beside me. "Wild . . . I knew Gen was hot for Rory, she'd been trailing him even during the Trials where she could. So despite what I felt, I knew I still had a chance. And I took a chance to protect you." He lifted his hand and brushed it down the side of my face, his ghostly touch sending a soft shiver through me. "But it wasn't Ruby who killed me."

I blinked up at him. "It wasn't?"

He shook his head and the smile finally slid away, turning into a sharp frown. "It was a mage who killed me. One I trusted with my life. When you opened up about Rory, we felt everything. I knew I ranked behind Rory. And behind me, far below, was Ethan. He didn't like that."

Colt reached up and touched me again even as the horror of what he was saying flowed through me. "He . . . Ethan killed you?"

The boy with the green eyes and the soft lips stared down at me. "Yes. That's exactly what I'm saying. Be careful, Wild. Please. As much as I care about you, I don't want to see you here with me any time soon. Deal?"

His body began to fade along with the burgundy mist. I held up my hand as if to high five him, and he did the same, our palms almost touching. "Deal."

Colt winked at me and then faded completely, along with the magic.

Wally let out a soft moan. "Wow, that was . . . draining, but so amazing. He really came to speak to you!"

I nodded. "You heard what he said?"

"About Ethan? Yeah . . . I wouldn't have thought it possible. I mean, cheating, yes. But actually killing Colt?"

She might not, but I could. If anyone got in the way of a Helix, death was a very distinct possibility. But still, the disappointment was there. That

Ethan could kill his best friend *did* shock me on some levels.

"Nothing we can do about Ethan right now," I said.

I pulled out the map that Gordy had given me of the jail where Frost was being held. Not that I needed it now. It was a giant square set on an island out in the harbor. An island the human world couldn't see, apparently, because I was pretty sure I would remember mention of a "Shadowspell Island Penitentiary."

I smoothed the map out. "Not very inventive with names, are they?"

Wally leaned over the map with me. "It's a giant square." Her words echoed my own thoughts.

The paper in my hands was layered, and I peeled up the first sheet. The next section was a more detailed look at the interior of the building, including entry points and windows. Another flip, and I was looking at a side view of the building. Four stories above ground and two stories below ground, though the underground section looked to be smaller than the footprint of the rest of the building.

I flipped another page, and I was looking at

guard stations. One more final flip, and my adrenaline spiked. I was suddenly feeling the urge to go now, to test myself against what I was staring at.

"It's levels and levels, by the looks of it. Each kind of supernatural in a different section." I turned the papers over again and realized how incomplete it was. It looked like a lot of information at a quick glance, but as soon as I saw that maze . . . "This would help if you had to go in, but there are a lot of unknowns. Has anyone ever broken in before? Successfully, that is?"

Wally shook her head. "Every attempt at escape has resulted in . . ." Her voice deepened. "Death."

Of course it had. Wally shrugged. "Far as I know, no one has ever tried to break in," She pause. "Were you really going in there to break us out?"

I stared at the map. "If I hadn't found you, yes. I wouldn't have had a choice, Wally. I couldn't leave you all there. You would have done the same for me."

"Of course we would!" Wally grabbed one of the apple pies.

Damn Frost. She knew me well enough to

know this challenge wouldn't scare me. Not one bit.

I was . . . excited to pit myself against a challenge like this even though I didn't have to now. Just like I had been excited to face the Culling Trials in a weird, adrenaline junkie sort of way.

"What about the Shadowkiller?" Wally picked at her fries. "He's still looking for you, isn't he?"

"Probably." I closed my eyes. "I'm doing all I can to block out his connection to me, which is why I had to do the same with ours. Apparently, it's all or nothing."

Wally leaned forward, her face catching the flashlight and looking even paler. "You mean you weren't trying to get rid of us?"

I shook my head, shocked she would even think that. "No! I know that we are stronger together, by a long shot. But I couldn't figure out how to only connect with one of you. I think . . . because Nicholas is my uncle there are some ties to him as well, which I suspect means he can find me if I'm not careful." I rubbed a hand over my face.

"Uncle Nicholas?"

"That's the Shadowkiller." I leaned my head back against the concrete.

"Holy cats," she whispered Pete's favorite saying and I found myself smiling.

"Cats on fire," I whispered back, missing him and the other guys fiercely in that moment, minus Ethan.

She laughed. "I wish they would hurry up."

I looked at her. "Me too. Are they any closer?"

Wally cocked her head to the side and closed her eyes. "No, they aren't. Weird. Maybe they stopped to eat?"

How much time had passed? An hour? No, not even that long. The urge to open up the connection between me and the guys was strong, but I had no doubt the second I did, Ash and my uncle would be on me. "Maybe they're hiding."

As soon as I said it, I knew it was true. Wally's eyes went wide. "They aren't hurt." She blinked and stared over my shoulder. "Rory . . . he's . . . someone is looking for them."

My heart did a terrible flip in my chest. "But they—"

"He is saying they need a distraction." Her eyes lost the glazed look. "They are calling to me, I have to go."

"Wait, what?" Calling to her? That sounded like a spell to me. "Is Ethan with them?"

"Yes." She was on her feet and moving to the door.

Bad idea, this was a bad idea. "Ethan could be somehow hijacking all this. You can't go. We have to figure out—"

She pushed me back, her power wrapping around me, stealing my air. "You stay. If I'm wrong you can come after us."

I struggled against the magic, struggled for air. "Wally, wait! It's not safe!"

Her burgundy magic dropped me and I scrambled up to my feet after her, but she was already out the door, moving faster than I'd ever seen her go. I put my hand between the sliding piece of concrete and the frame to stop it from closing behind her, but it didn't slow for me.

I yanked my hand out at the last second, then banged a fist on the smooth, hard surface. "Wally!" Damn it, if she didn't come back, if something happened to them, I was going to be in serious trouble. Stuck in a crypt, buried alive. How the hell did she think I was going to be able to go after them if she didn't come back?

"Wally!" I yelled her name, the sound bouncing off the walls. Damn it. Again the urge to check on my crew was intense. But I couldn't do anything unless I found a way out of here first.

The flashlight took that moment to flicker. "Are you kidding me?"

I picked it up from the floor, turned it off, and stashed it in my pack.

The darkness was total and complete, and I just closed my eyes as I slid to the floor.

"You better hurry up, Wally," I muttered under my breath.

Minutes ticked by, hell, it could have been hours for all I could tell. That kind of darkness seemed to distort time, slowing it down and speeding it up. I slowed my breathing. Despite my worry, the sheer exhaustion overwhelmed me. This was as good a place as any for a nap, and it wasn't long before I dozed off.

I had no idea how much time had passed when a thump of something heavy sent my hand toward one of the new knives before I was fully awake. I pulled the blade slowly so that no sound rasped off the steel or the sheath.

Opening my eyes, I fully expected there to be nothing to see but black nothingness. I stood and ran my hands over the crypt walls, feeling for something that could have made the thump, even though I knew that nothing was there.

The tips of my fingers slid over an indent, just the slightest of marks in the wall. I paused and let my fingers follow the flow of the lines. Circular, around and around to a central point that depressed under my finger.

Ooops.

A sudden low green glow that ran around the edges of one of the coffin recesses directly across from me was as bright as daylight to my eyes and about as unexpected.

I stood and took a step toward the opening. The green light traveled all along the edges, lighting up the space like a 3-D image. I put the tip of my knife against the part of the green line closest to me and the bottom of the recess sunk, revealing a black opening leading into the bowels of the graveyard. That had to be the thump I'd heard—the cement covering sliding open.

Wind blew up and out of the opening, ruffling my hair and bringing me a smell I couldn't pinpoint. Acrid, sharp, a little pungent, a little coppery. I wrinkled my nose, wishing Pete was here with that nose of his to identify what I was smelling.

"*Come.*" The whispered moan of a word sent goose bumps up and down my spine. But no warning. Just that one word traveling on another gust of cool wind.

I stepped back. "Yeah, that's a hard pass."

"*Come.*" This time there was some serious demand in the voice, along with an oomph of power that crawled across my skin. I took another step back, which pretty much put me against the far wall. Not enough room between me and that freaky black hole, and the freakier voice that was getting all pushy.

"Nope, I'm good. You go on by yourself. I'm just going to sit here. Quietly. Doing nothing. Causing no trouble. Not touching anything else." I pulled my second knife out as my back tingled like sharp little daggers were dancing up and down it.

The green glow intensified. "*Come. Now.*" Power lashed out around me, and my eyes fuzzed over for a moment. I wobbled but stayed standing, back pressed against the concrete wall for support.

"Still passing." I shook my head and blinked rapidly to clear my vision. "You know, maybe try the next crypt over? See if they have any takers."

The clatter of wood against cement, like sticks falling to the ground, came next.

Only it wasn't wood. I blinked again, not fully sure of what I was seeing at first.

A hoof curled over the edge of the opening—black and solid and attached to a leg bone bare of any flesh—and a critter pulled itself halfway up. Surprise, surprise, it wasn't a human skull that came out of the glowing darkness. A ram's head popped up and over the edge, the curling horns sweeping backward, an upside-down Y burned into the front of its skull.

"Who the hell sends a sheep skeleton to do their dirty work?" I yelled at it, part horrified, part amused. "Especially going after a farm girl!"

It turned its head toward me, blood dripping from the empty eyeholes.

So much for the amusement factor. Well, this was a turn I'd not counted on.

I held my blades up. "Let's dance, sheep."

9

WALLY

I ran from the marble gardens back the way Wild and I had come, dodging a few pedestrians, but there weren't actually that many people kicking around. Rory said they needed a distraction. But I was questioning myself now about leaving Wild behind.

What if the guys were in bigger trouble than I could handle? I put a hand to my head. "What the hell was I thinking?"

It was well after midnight now. Though the time from when Wild had been taken by the Shadowkiller to now had gone by both fast and slow. From what I could feel, the guys weren't too far. But to run off like that . . . it wasn't like me. I knew it.

What if Ethan had done something?

I let out a slow breath. “I’ll make this right.”

I had only one goal. I would find the guys and take them to Wild. Then we’d all be together, and we’d have a sixty-seven percent better chance of survival. Maybe even seventy percent if we were very lucky.

At least, that was what I told myself. Because if I was being honest, the numbers were not in our favor, not at all. Two Chameleons were trying to control or kill Wild (or possibly one, then the other), we were being hunted by the Helix family on behalf of Frost, and we’d already lost Colt. To Ethan. And now maybe he’d turned on us again.

My throat tightened, feeling his death hit me once more. Feeling him die and not being able to stop it like we had with Ethan.

“I should have let you die in the Culling Trials,” I said to myself. He’d fooled us more times than I wanted to admit. All because he was strong and handsome and a good liar.

On a main street once more, I did a slow turn, searching for that sensation inside my head that was the guys.

Pete’s shifter energy was the first I found, and he wasn’t far. I’d pull him aside as soon as I could and tell him we had to get away from Ethan. Orin and Gregory would back me up, too, I was sure. And so would Rory.

A tight smile on my face, I ran down the street, taking turns almost blindly until I found them.

Only they weren't hiding and they weren't alone.

I slid to a stop as I stared at the Shade with the bright red hair, Mr. Helix right next to her. Ethan was beside him, his chin to his chest. Rory was flat out on the ground at the Shade's feet, her boot on the middle of his back.

Pete turned and saw me. "RUN, WALLY!"

He was too late, though. I spun and ran face first into the twin's oversized muscled chest, bouncing off and hitting the ground hard. He reached down and dragged me to my feet, quickly tying my hands behind my back with something that felt like a zip tie.

"Zap straps, only pansies use zap straps," Gregory growled, and Mr. Helix cuffed him in the back of the head, sending him to the ground, unconscious.

"Come on, little necro," Dallin said. "Boss wants to talk to you."

He dragged me forward. I tried to bring my

magic to me, but fear clogged my mind and hampered my ability. Fear and the realization that I'd walked into a trap. No, worse than that: I'd run into it.

I managed to slow my breathing enough to check on Rory. He was still alive, but he was out cold, and I didn't think he'd be waking up anytime soon; there was a lot of blood pooling around him. If he didn't get help soon he'd be joining Colt.

Ruby laughed and wiped her knuckles clear of something. Blood maybe? "He's quick. A few more years, and he'll be faster than Rufus."

"He's not getting a few more years," Mr. Helix said. "Leave him here to die."

Ruby sighed. "Despite what you think, you are not in charge."

His face tightened and she smiled as she reached over and dusted off his shirt as if we weren't even there. "The boss wants them as bait, and what the boss wants, she gets." Her smirk widened. "Think of it as a two-for-one deal, if you will. Because wherever Wild goes . . . well, let's just say she brings all the boys to our yard."

I swallowed hard and found my voice. "She won't do it. She won't follow."

Ruby looked at me and licked her lips. "Oh, but

she will. Especially if she feels one of you die. Don't you think?"

She glanced down at Rory and pulled a knife. "One more death. To make sure."

"He's not connected to her," Orin said quickly. "He's not in her crew."

Ruby turned to him. "No? Then why is he here?"

"He followed us," Pete said. "Thought he'd get points with the Sandman for bringing us back."

Ruby looked down at Rory's still body. "So eager to die. Fine. Then I'll just have to kill one of you." She flipped her knife in her hand and shot a look at Pete.

Not Pete.

"NO!" I yelled the word, knowing what any one of our deaths would do to Wild. Knowing that my own feelings for Pete were . . . complicated. "No . . . I'll . . . I'll take you to her. Just don't hurt him!"

Ruby stood up straight, turned, and looked at me. "What? My understanding is she has cut off all her connections, so you can't know where she is."

How in the seven hells did this Shade know that about Wild? Who'd been blabbing?

I shook my head. "I know where she is."

Orin groaned. "Don't do this, Wally."

My throat tightened. “She wouldn’t forgive any of us for dying on her. Or for letting Ruby kill one of us.”

The other boys knew what I meant. Even Ethan, who stood there next to his dad, not tied up. Not bound.

“Don’t look at me like that, Wally,” he said.

“You mean like you looked at Colt before you killed him? Like you didn’t just draw me here with a spell so that we could all be captured?” I snapped. Ethan paled, and the others turned to him, anger etched in their faces. “How could you kill your best friend? We were right to cast you out the first time. Don’t think we’ll make that mistake again.”

Ethan closed his eyes. “It isn’t what you think.”

Mr. Helix dropped a hand onto his son’s shoulder. “We are winners in this world, and winners don’t play with street rats. He’s going to be part of the winning side. Finally. As he should have been all along.”

Ruby snapped her fingers at the twins. “Take the others, drop them into the prison. I’ll bring this one if she fails to find the young Chameleon.”

Orin, Pete, and Gregory fought against the zap straps, but they didn’t break and there was nothing I could do. I looked at Pete, silently asking him if he could shift and he shook his head. "The straps are spelled," he said. "Ethan . . . he knocked us all out before they even showed up."

That explained why they hadn't moved in all that time. They'd been asleep.

"I'm trying to keep you alive!" Ethan yelled, and his father hit him, backhanding him hard across the face, dropping him to his knees.

"Shut your mouth."

Ruby pointed at me. "You and I, we're going to have a girls' night with our friend Wild. If I can find her and kill her, then you might live a little longer. Maybe Frost will even want to take you on. Make you your father's replacement. Theo is getting old."

I shook my head, shock turning my mind and heart numb. "No, no that's not true. It's not possible. He's not . . . he's not with Frost. You're lying!" Frost already had two people from the House of Night . . . how big was her crew? How many people had she drawn off?

My father was always so busy, we rarely spent time together. And when we did? I thought of the occasions when I'd failed to raise the dead or communicate easily with a ghost. He'd seemed disappointed and then . . . relieved.

Ruby laughed as she tightened a hand on my arm until the bones ground against one another. "Did you never wonder why he didn't train you? Why he told you that you were weak? I see it now, and so does Frost. He tried to protect you. But there is no 'keeping safe' from a woman like Frost."

She gave me a little shake as she propelled me forward. I tried to turn to look at the boys, to see where they were going, but they were already gone. They'd left Rory on the ground, injured and bleeding. He'd die without help.

"No, my father—"

"Thought he was protecting you by presenting you as weak, which meant you went under the radar for years. Clever of him." She patted me on the head with her free hand. "But not anymore."

I forced my feet to walk in the general direction of the House of Night, my mind racing with numbers. No, not numbers, a single number.

Hundred percent that Wild was still in my family crypt.

Hundred percent that she would be caught by Ruby.

I didn't see any way she could get herself out of this.

Unless . . . I closed my eyes and let my feet guide me as I whispered his name.

"Tommy Johnson."

"What did you say?" Ruby gave me another shake, and I opened my eyes. Tommy stood to the side of me, faded but there.

"Warn Wild." I mouthed the two words, but Tommy shook his head.

"She can't see me without you."

Frustration welled in me so strongly that I felt as though I were choking. Ahead of us was the marble gardens. If I didn't figure out something, I was putting Wild right into a trap. A trap that I had created by falling for Ethan's trick. One chance left.

I sent my energy toward the crypt, pushing my magic into the stone. I was in danger, and while I'd never seen it, there was another way out. It just had to open for Wild. And give her a chance.

"What are you doing?" Ruby shook me yet again.

"I'm trying to connect with her. To make sure she is still there."

The connection between me and Wild was a two-way street when it was open. Strong emotions seemed to overpower everything—perhaps even the closed-down connection—and the terror riding me was as good as anything to use. With all I had, I tried to send her a message.

Get out of there, Wild. If you can sense this at all, get out of there!

10

WILD

The sheep skeleton with the ram's head hopped fully out of the crypt and held out a hoof to me. Pointing at me.

I kept both knives at the ready. "What do you want, fluff butt?"

The ram's head tipped toward the empty black hole it had just crawled out of, and I was seriously doubting some of my life choices up to that point.

There was nowhere for me to go, no door to escape through. I pointed my blades a little lower, closer to the ram's empty eye sockets. "No. Seriously, no." As if denying a walking sheep skeleton would have any effect on the thing. Then again, maybe it did.

Its bones rattled as it sagged, and I let out a

breath. Stupid of me to let my guard down. I'd worked with sheep before. The cheeky bastards always let you think you'd won right before—

The sheep skeleton lunged at me headfirst, pinning my lower body to the wall. Its strength was no different than a living ram, only this one had something a normal sheep did not.

Two skeletal arms shot out of its ribcage and grabbed for me. Bony fingers tore at my clothes as it wrestled to keep my arms down. I drove a knee up into the neck of the critter, but there was no wind to knock out of it, no flesh to bruise, and the sheep skeleton didn't so much as grunt. All it did was lift its head back and ram me again. Slamming me hard.

I slashed at the head with one knife, and the blade glanced off the horns. The ram reared up and drove its head toward mine. I ducked, but a tip of one horn caught the flesh of my cheek, tearing it open and sending a trickle of warmth down my face and neck.

Driving a foot into the front leg of the sheep, I snapped the bone in half, throwing it off balance. Only I couldn't get free of the arms and we pirouetted to the side, spinning slowly toward the opening.

"No, no! I don't want to dance with you after all!"

The door behind me began to slowly open, and a strange sensation welled in my mind, as if my skull was filling with water. Someone was trying to make themselves heard through our connection. "Kinda busy here!" I hollered. "Sheep problems!"

The pressure increased, and suddenly I knew who was outside the door. And she was scared.

"Wally!" I screamed for her as the ram let go, backed up and jammed me in the guts. I fell into the black hole, and it hopped in after me.

"Wild! Ruby has us!" Wally screamed.

Her words slammed into me a split second before I hit the floor, landing on my hip and side. I wasn't sure I'd even heard them out loud.

The wind whooshed out of me and whatever light had been there a moment before dissipated as the crypt opening closed over my head. I rolled, throwing the now limp ram's head skeleton off me.

Utter and complete blackness surrounded me, and I struggled to calm my breathing.

Ruby had my friends. Which meant Frost had my friends.

"Damn it," I growled as I pulled my flashlight out of my bag and flicked it on. The beam was dim, but it was there, and as I panned it around the area, I realized there were no stairs leading up to the space over me.

Something hammered on the stone above my head.

Wally was in danger.

I had no choice. I dared to open the connection to just her, and Wally's emotions and thoughts roared through me.

Ruby found the boys before me. Ethan helped them. Rory is hurt bad. The others are being taken to the jail. Probably me too.

Wally wanted me to run. I saw the street where the boys had been snagged. Where Rory was even now lying on the ground, possibly bleeding out.

A string of curses flew from my mouth as I sat there and struggled not to scream. Nothing was going right. Nothing. But I couldn't let her know that.

I sent her a single calming thought and spoke the words out loud. "I'll find you, Wally. Just go along with them for now."

The pounding above my head stopped, and I closed off the connection to Wally. I had to. Because in that brief moment, I'd felt others searching for me. Back into the grain silo all the connections went, and I slammed that mental door closed once again.

Ash and my uncle were still out there, of that I had no doubt. And their eyes had turned toward me in that brief moment of connection with Wally.

Behind me, the scrabble of bones spun me around. The beam of my flashlight caught the edge of the ram's skull as it pulled itself onto its three functional legs.

Pointing the beam at the animated skeleton, I swept the area until I found both knives and retrieved them. Not that they'd done me much good. I mean . . . how did you kill something that was both dead and had no proper flesh or muscle?

"Head shots," I said. "I'll take your horns and cut off your head if you come any closer."

The beastly skeleton bobbled to the side and then started off down a dark tunnel, dragging one set of its fingernails along the cement sidewall with a steady scratching, the cloven hooves making a rather fine clopping noise. The leg I'd broken seemed to have fixed itself.

Then it snapped its fingers at me, crooking one of them in the universal come-hither motion. Now it wanted me to follow?

Dripping water, the smell of mold and rot, and

my skin was itching with the need to move. It was apparent that the ram wasn't the least bit concerned whether I would follow.

There was no other way than the tunnel it had gone down. Awesome, just how I'd hoped my night would go.

I started after it, keeping both the light and my knife at eye level. I didn't like how quiet this was, how . . . seemingly safe. I mean, sure, I was trapped in an underground crypt, but where was the flooding water? The hordes of spiders? Or even a more aggressive skeleton? None of it made sense.

"Where are you leading me?" I called out into the darkness, and the scratching of the fingers on the wall stopped.

I stopped too. I had no wish to snuggle up to some sheepish skeleton dude.

A light bobbed up ahead of me, and I pinned myself to the wall, pulling the shadows around me as I slowed my breathing.

"I know you are here, Shade. I can smell you, and more than that, I can smell the blood on your face."

Smell.

Vampire or shifter? He'd gone for the blood so . . .

"Vampire," I called out, "you want to dance?"

"No, I do not. I am far too old to play these games." The light bobbled closer, and an old man bent at the waist with long white hair and a beard came into view. He didn't look like much of a threat, but a vampire was a vampire, was a vampire.

"You can get out past me, but you must answer a riddle first. My master Theo has decreed this is the way." He slowed until he was about fifteen feet away, give or take a few inches.

"A riddle," I deadpanned.

"That is the cost of escaping this crypt. My master has asked me to protect the secret exit, and while I'm not sure he even remembers putting me down here with my familiar, I am very much still bound by those rules." He groaned a little as he lowered himself to the ground.

This was ridiculous.

I put my knife away and sprinted past him. I didn't have time for riddles.

My foot lined up with him, and then I was flat on my face with a hand wrapped tightly around my ankle. "You get one warning," he said with his raspy voice. "One only, and then I can kill you. Let me tell you, the taste of true blood would be a blessing after all these years alone, feasting on rats."

Once more, I was sucking wind hard, trying to find my breath. Before I could consider getting to my feet, I was thrown backward down the hall, my flashlight bouncing off the wall and blinking out.

"Are you ready for the riddle?" the vampire asked.

"My friends are in danger. I don't have time for a riddle!" I yelled at him as I got to my feet. The only pinprick of light was from his lantern, which cast a sickly glow over him and the area closest to his seat.

"Then you must answer quickly. Besides, there is a time limit on the riddle itself. One minute."

One minute? He had to be kidding.

Sweet baby jeebus, what I wouldn't give to have Gregory with me right then. Or Orin. They both had a logical side that allowed them to think about things in ways I couldn't.

"And you'll let me go. Pass right by when I give you the right answer?"

"Yes, of course. Those are the rules here. Much as I hate them," he grumbled, fumbling around with his clothing. I blinked at the glimmer of something small and metallic. Like a pen.

What the hell did a vampire need a pen for down in a crypt? Hopefully that wasn't the riddle, because I had no damn idea.

"What is that?"

He held his light up and clutched at the item. "It's mine."

"What is it?" I asked again.

"Mine," he growled. "Now the riddle."

Interesting.

The old vampire cleared his throat. "The more you take, the more you leave behind." He paused and drew a sucking breath through his teeth. "What am I?"

My mind took an immediate left turn and blanked out. The more you take . . . the more you leave?

"How many times can I answer?" I asked.

"As many as you like in the minute," he said, and then he laughed. "You Shades are not smart enough even for an easy riddle like this one. I am hungry, though, so it will be my pleasure to tell you when you fail."

Balls, he might be right on the not smart enough to answer this riddle portion. So I just started throwing words out rapid-fire style. "Trees, rocks, time, love, hate, breathing—"

"No to all of them."

I wracked my brain. "Knowledge. Books."

"Still no."

The more you take. I paced the small space.

"You have fifteen seconds left."

My feet stilled. My *feet*.

The answer was right there on the tip of my brain. I could feel it. I was not a dumbass like Shaw. I was smarter than the average Shade. I had to be. Steps. I took another one toward him. "Footsteps."

He sucked in a sharp breath. "Correct. Damn you."

I shouldn't have been so damn happy, but I was. I adjusted my bag on my back and broke into a jog. "Adios, mi amigo."

"I think . . . not. My hunger is too much, and while I will be punished, I cannot let you go." He lunged for me, but this time I was ready for it. I went straight up, straddling the narrow hall like I'd straddled the bus seats what seemed like a lifetime ago. Two days? Had it only been two days since the Culling Trials had ended?

He slammed into the wall headfirst, and I leaped forward, snatching up his lantern as I went.

A part of me wanted to grab for his metal precious, but I left it alone.

A screeching roar echoed through the tunnel, and I sprinted, barely slowing to take the turns that wove me through the underground of the graveyard. Slowly, slowly the tunnel narrowed even as it rose.

Behind me was the clatter of the ram's feet on the stones and the snarling hiss of what I could only assume was a starving vampire.

I took another turn, crouching for the low ceiling, and hit a dead end. "Are you serious?" I hissed. The wall in front of me was solid stone. I tried to stand, and my head brushed nothing but dirt that rained down around me in a pattering of stones and dust.

I blinked and put a hand over my head, clawing at the dirt. More fell. Everything here was loose.

"Shit." Up it was then, the only way out.

I put the lantern down, grabbed both knives, and began to dig at the ground above my head. More and more fell, but the sound of my newfound friends was also drawing closer.

I had to get the hell out of here.

Like now.

I redoubled my efforts, dragging my weapons through the soil as fast as I could.

Not fast enough.

The ram's head slammed into my upper thigh, driving me to the ground. I kicked out with the un-rammed leg.

"I hate sheep! You stink!" The ram slammed its horns into me again, pinning me to the ground.

The lantern was on its side, the light wobbling, which only made the image of the starving vampire creeping toward me that much freakier. Limbs moving like they were detached at the joints, the crawling vampire turned itself upside down and then rolled its head around to look at me right side up.

"Feast day, pet," he whispered and flashed his fangs.

With a grunt, I grabbed the ram and threw it off, tumbling it right into its vampire friend. I stood and drove both hands up through the ground, feeling the open air.

Fingers wrapped around mine and pulled as the vampire latched onto my calf. I kicked him with my other foot, and his teeth tore through the flesh.

"No, no!" he screamed. "I am starving, starving! Let me have her!"

I was pulled upward and out of the ground, and the sudden silence was as unnerving as the catacombs. No more screaming vampire, but no sound of my rescuer either.

I blinked and shook my head to get the dirt out of my face, hoping it was who I thought it might be. "Rory?"

A sigh and the sound of leathery wings. "I think not, young Shade."

11

The gargoyle let go of me, and I rolled across the ground, missing a tombstone before driving up to my feet. Around us, the graveyard was silent. Not even the distant sound of horns or traffic. Magic was my first guess. Which slightly amused me since I'd only really known magic to be a real thing for about ten days.

Ash stared at me. "What were you doing in the necromancer's crypt?"

I countered him. "How did you find me?"

"You opened yourself to your friend, and I knew you were somewhere near here." He smiled. "Let us go before the vampire decides to join us—"

"No." I settled into a fighting stance. And then I realized that I had an opportunity here, one that I might not get again. “What does my uncle want with me? To see me drained like Frost? He said he wanted to steal my friends too.”

Ash shook his head. “Nothing like what Frost wants with them.”

“To hurt me or my friends?”

He didn’t answer right away. “He . . . is not the young man I knew when he came through the school. The power he has changed him, but he is not like Frost. He is trying to make things right.”

“But he’s a killer.”

The gargoyle tipped his head. “As are you. Unless Jared fell by another’s hand?”

My jaw ticked at the comparison.

Ash smiled. “Perhaps you are not so different from your uncle after all. Perhaps he is just . . . misunderstood.”

I snorted. “I don’t think so. My mother died to keep us safe from him.”

Behind me, the ground crumbled as a bony hand shot out. I turned and kicked it, snapping fingers on the undead, starving vampire as if kicking off the head of a thistle back home.

“Something he deeply regrets that he wasn’t able to stop from happening.” Ash tipped his head toward me. "But we must go. Ruby will be hunting the graveyard now."

He held a hand out to me, and I brought both knives up. "No."

The tension between us grew. The vampire again pushed his fingers out. This time I cut them off with a swipe of my right blade.

"What about a deal?" Ash said slowly, as if listening to something in his right ear. He even tipped his head that way. "A deal, yes, that might work. She is a clever one if she got by Barnaby."

Barnaby. That had to be the starving vampire below.

I moved to put a tombstone between us as he shifted his attention back to me. "Why would I make a deal with you? Why wouldn't I just . . ." I was going to say *kill you*, but then that would only reinforce that he was right—that I was just like my uncle. "Leave. Run again."

Ash folded his wings tightly to his body. "Because you are going to be taken either way. By Nicholas, or perhaps by Frost, who will do nothing but harm you, and who, if my sources are correct, has now taken your friends. You need help. He is offering you that much. If you come with me now."

Every muscle in me screamed to run, to find

Wally, Pete, Orin, Gregory, and even stupid Ethan. More than that, I had to find Rory.

"Yes, Frost has taken my friends." I bit the words out. "We've taken her on before. And we beat her. We can beat her again."

"You are no fool, Wild. You know when you are outmatched. The first time you surprised her. And she did not have all those who are tied to her with her. You were lucky, and I believe you know that." He paused. "You were very, very lucky."

Two hands surged out of the dirt along with the top of Barnaby's head. I spun and slammed the heel of my boot into his skull, jamming him back into the ground. One arm waved around and snagged my pants, but I swept a blade down, slashing his arm. A howl ripped up from the ground, and I took another step back, even though it put me closer to Ash.

The gargoyle watched me closely. "Perhaps, in time, you'll be able to do all that you set your mind to, but you do not know everything. There is much for you to learn." Ash folded his arms as if he had all the time in the world. Which I suppose he did. I was the one in a damn hurry. "You cannot save your friends on your own. This is not the Culling Trials. This is not even the academy. This is the real world, and it is no place for an untrained Chameleon Shade and her companions. You will die. And then your friends will die. Are you willing to throw all those lives away?" He searched my face. "And do you think Frost will stop there if you keep thwarting her? How long before she looks to your family farm? To your siblings and your father?"

The air around us tensed, because I had to make this choice whether I liked it or not. The grave was quiet now. Apparently, Barnaby had given up.

I hated that the gargoyle was right. Frost would not relent. And my family that I'd gone to the Culling Trials to protect? They'd be in danger. My father was in no condition to protect anyone, and the twins were still kids. I'd do anything to keep them safe.

Like eating ashes out of a fire, I choked out the words. "What kind of deal are you offering?"

Ash smiled, though there was a tinge of sadness to it. "See, you are a clever one. The deal is this. Nicholas and I will help you get your friends from the prison. But when they are freed from their cages, you will peacefully come with us. No more fighting."

Peacefully.

"What about my friends? Nicholas wanted them too."

"He has changed his mind and will take just you if that is what it must be," Ash said.

I ground my teeth while I considered this. I could almost feel Rory slipping away. "All of my friends, and that includes Rory getting help. I can't leave him," I said.

Ash nodded. "You have my word, on pain of death. You may open your connection to your friends now. It will make it easier for us to find them."

He turned, and I did just that, flinging that giant grain silo open and grabbing hold of the golden threads attaching me to my friends. The bonds between us were stronger than ever, even with the distance between us.

East, my friends were east of here, and the pull from them was steady as well as the shock they felt that I was connecting with them. Wally had been taken far away already, and was with the boys now too.

Ash was right about needing to find them. I wouldn't have thought they'd already be that far east.

"Rory was on 17th Street, near a smoke shop." I hurried past him, wishing I could feel Rory the same way I could feel the rest of my crew inside my head.

And then I thought about him kissing Gen, and I wasn't so sure that was a good idea. Yeah, strike that. Of course, I was just thinking these things because I didn't want to consider the possibility that we would arrive too late. That I'd lose him the way I'd lost Tommy and Colt.

In the back of my head, Gregory, Pete, and Orin were freaking the shit out. Wally was trying to calm them, and Ethan . . . he was quiet. And not with the others at all. He was in the opposite direction.

I twisted around as we came to an intersection. "Ethan helped Frost."

"I suppose it is possible," Ash said, though his tone said otherwise. "More likely his father has something to do with it."

I had to shake it off. Ethan was the least of my worries right then. Through the connection, I could tell he was still suffering from the sickness, but it felt like he was healing. I could almost see him turn his head toward me at the realization we were connected once more. So much for cutting him off from the crew as I'd tried to do.

Something I was going to do as soon as I could. Maybe killing him would do the trick? I mean, it was only fair considering he'd killed Colt. Yet the idea of killing Ethan didn't appeal to me. Not that I loved him, it was more like . . . I couldn't believe that all we'd been through together meant nothing to him. Again he'd turned on us. I wasn't sure that killing him would make any of it better.

I gave myself a mental shake and put all that aside for now.

The only one of my friends who was in danger of actually dying right that second was Rory.

Picking up speed, I didn't wait for Ash to stick close, and a moment later, he flew above me, the push of air from his wings tickling at my face. I glanced at the next street. One more to reach 17th.

I turned the corner and bolted down the nearly empty road, my body tensing as my awareness of danger grew incrementally. But I didn't slow. I couldn't. Not with Rory somewhere around here needing help.

From above, Ash called down to me. "They put a shield on him so no human could find him."

And so that he would die for sure. "I'm going to

kill her." So much for not being like my uncle. In the last few minutes, I'd promised myself I'd kill two different people. To be fair, I wasn't even sure which 'her' I meant. Ruby or Frost. "Them," I amended. Maybe three people then.

I slowed my feet and narrowed my eyes, doing what I could to look through the shadows that had been cast everywhere. Not natural shadows but ones cast by Ruby.

Tricks of the trade that I didn't truly understand, but I had to figure them out if I was to find Rory.

"Come on," I whispered as I reached out and touched one of the shadows. It stuck to my fingers as if I had glue on the tips. I flicked it off, and it slid back to where it had been.

"Try again," Ash said gently. God, why couldn't people just be like they seemed? He seemed kind, but he was attached to the Shadowkiller. Ethan had always pretty much seemed like a douche, but there'd been times when he was a *likeable* douche.

I dug into the shadows with both hands and took hold of them. A sting, like biting ants, rippled up and over my skin as I yanked the shadows away. This could all be a trap, but I didn't care. I was going to get to Rory if it was the last damn thing I did.

Rory was somewhere in here, and he was . . . dying. I didn't have to be connected to him like I was to my crew to know he was in trouble.

"Damn it," I growled as sweat broke out along my brow. The biting feeling intensified as I peeled the shadows back, one by one. By the time I'd removed them all, my hands were burning, bright red as if I'd had them inside a fire.

But I found him. I found Rory.

He lay face down on the cement, far too still for my liking. Rushing to his side, I dropped to my knees and pressed my ear to his back while I worked to find a pulse in his neck, wincing as my skin brushed against his shirt.

I held my breath and tried to still my own heart, waiting for his to thrum in my ears.

Silence.

Then a beat, finally, but he was still alive, and it would have to be enough to get him through this. "It's bad. I need to call for help." I fumbled with my bag, my fingers aching as I finally managed to pull out the radio, flicking it on to hear the Sandman's voice.

"Goddamn it, Johnson, answer me!"

I depressed the button. "Nice to hear from you too."

He took a sharp breath. "Where the hell are you?"

"17th and Driftwood, just past the old smoke shop. Bring a healer." I clicked the radio off and stuffed it back in my pack. Carefully, wincing, I slid my hands under his shirt until I found the wound I knew would be on his body somewhere. I found it, a warm wet spot right in the middle of his back. I pulled the thick pack of bandages from my bag, folded two and pressed them against the wound with one hand. Then I ran my fingers over the rest of his body. Because if I'd wanted to incapacitate a Shade as good as Rory there wouldn't be just one wound. There would be at least two or maybe even three to make sure he didn't get up and come after me.

"Why not just kill him?" Ash muttered. "That would destroy you. What is her game?"

A second warm wet spot on the inside of Rory's right thigh stopped my hand. "Ash, can you bind up his leg? There's gauze in the bag. But you're wrong, it wouldn't destroy me."

Tommy's death hadn't. It had hardened me, made me less willing to negotiate.

The gargoyle crouched beside me, took a strip of gauze out of my bag and wrapped it around Rory's upper thigh with a smooth dexterity that surprised me given those big claws of his.

"You have excellent control of your emotions," Ash said, "especially considering who this is to you. But I want you to think on the fact that this could be a trap."

"Already have considered it," I said. "But if I were Ruby or Frost, would I want to send *me* into a rage there would be no coming back from? Because that's what would happen if Rory died. They want me worried, distracted, but not out for blood. That's why they didn't kill him."

It was a different kind of trap.

A trap of the heart and mind. And I would have to leave him once help arrived if I was going to get to Wally and the others. I would have to, and I would do it. Didn't matter how much I wanted to stay with him.

I kept the pressure on Rory's back and continued checking his body for other injuries. "Help me roll him onto his side."

I chose not to respond to his comment about my emotions, because he was right and he was wrong. My fear for Rory was through the freaking roof. If it had been *me* in trouble, that would have been another discussion. I struggled to truly be afraid for my own hide. Live or die, that was life every day in my world, more so now than ever before.

But my friends and family? I would do anything for them.

Frost knew it. She knew my weakness.

Ash helped me tip Rory over so I could run my fingers over his face, neck, chest, and belly. I paused to the left of his belly button, feeling the thinnest of puncture wounds oozing with what I first thought was pus. No, not pus, some sort of liquid that did not belong in him. "He's been given something. An injection of some sort."

I pulled my finger away and smelled the oozing clear liquid. "I don't know what it is. Smells like licorice."

Ash took my hand and wiped it across the ground. "Poison. Most likely it is one of Ruby's concoctions, so it would be best if your help for this one arrives soon."

A groan rippled out of Rory and I leaned close. "Hang on, help is coming."

"Wild. Tell her . . . tell her I love her." Blood burbled over his lips and I turned him on his side.

I thought my heart couldn't knot up more, but I was wrong. I swallowed my own hurt, swallowed it deep and nodded while I struggled to speak around the tension in my throat. "You can tell her yourself. You aren't dying."

As if on cue, the screech of tires rippled through the air. Ash pinned himself to the wall behind me, blending in with the stone of the building with a burst of his blue misting magic.

I looked up to see the Sandman followed by two others. One was the director of the House of Claw, his eyes sweeping the area; the other was Mara.

Sandman reached me first, and I quickly rattled off the injuries and the needle mark. "Mara, you can save him, right?"

She crouched beside me with a wince, and the hand she pressed to her own belly reminded me she'd been stabbed not all that long ago—a few hours at most. "I think we are here just in time. The poison means I need to be careful. If you hadn't noticed that injection, the healing I gave him would have actually set the poison off. A clever trick of the House of Shade." Her hands replaced mine on Rory's wounds, and I stood and stepped back to give them room.

The Sandman glanced up at me. "Where are the others?"

The House of Claw director sniffed the air. "Something else is here. House of Unmentionables, I think."

I smiled at the Sandman, really smiled, even though I knew he was going to be pissed at me when he saw who I was with. Or maybe that was why I was smiling. Nothing was more fun than setting off the most dangerous Shade the world had ever seen. "I'm getting them back, Rufus. Take care of Rory for me. Please." I looked down at Rory, wanting to . . . no. He wasn't mine and I had to get that through my thick skull.

"A gargoyle, we've got company," the House of Claw director growled as he began to shift.

I took a step back. The Sandman stared at me, his aviators still firmly in place, but I could feel the weight of his gaze. "Find them, then. But hurry up about it. We've got other problems. The sickness is spreading faster."

I saluted him as Ash grabbed me from behind and launched into the air between the buildings on either side of us.

The cold, wet night was finally getting to me, and the shivering started in my middle and spread outward. So, I asked questions to distract myself from the cold. "Do you know him too? I mean as a teacher?"

"The Sandman? Yes, I know Rufus. He is very strait-laced. Mara gave him a reason to be soft, which has allowed him to be even stronger than before."

"Not complicated at all," I said as I took in the city below us. Ash was taking us east, at least, but really high up. Even if I'd been willing to break my word, I didn't want to fall from this height. No doubt the gargoyle knew it.

"It isn't complicated. Love makes us stronger, young Shade. Some see it as a weakness. But it is not," he said. "Remember that."

"You mean like how my friends are being used and hurt to control me?" I said, unable to keep the bitterness out of my voice. "That's because Frost knows I care about them. It's my fault."

"Of course, there is always a chance of that happening, especially in our world. People being hurt, that is." Ash shrugged and tipped his wings so we angled downward. "But that is not the point. The point is that when bad things happen to us—and they always do, none are immune to them—love is what can see us through. Our friends are the ones who are there to help us keep our heads above the cold winds that would sweep us off course."

I frowned as we drew closer and closer to the ground. The water was off to the side, and in front of us lay a burned-out building site. Call me crazy, but I'd bet good money that I was looking at Pier 36. The House of Shade without any of its former glory.

And right next to it? The man who had brought our whole world crumbling down. The man I'd agreed to go with *peacefully* when this was all done.

The Shadowkiller.

12

WALLY

The prison really wasn't as bad as I'd thought it was going to be. Not that I'd really given it much thought until the moment I realized we were going to be stuffed there. The walls were slick gray, smooth like glass or ice, and the temperature wasn't hot or cold, just right in the middle. If I closed my eyes, I could easily imagine I was floating in a dream without anything tickling at my senses. No smells, no outside sounds—

"You think Wild will be able to get us out?" Pete asked, breaking through my thoughts. "Not that I don't think she's badass, but this . . ."

I knew what he meant. This was next-level, off-the-charts crazy hard. "She'll come after she finds

Rory. She can get help from others, possibly. Maybe the Sandman could help her?"

Orin sighed. "She could just go back to the school and ask them to search the penitentiary for us."

"And who is at the school? You aren't just a pair of dumb fangs. Use your head!" Gregory snapped as he paced the small space around the edges, trailing his hands over the slick surface. "Ethan's father is there, and the House of Wonder is controlling this whole situation. She can't go for help. There isn't any. Even the directors of the other houses wouldn't want to take on Helix."

"Ethan won't be of any help either," Pete said. "I can't . . . I can't believe he killed Colt. Or that he just wrapped us up like Thanksgiving turkeys for them!"

"I can," Gregory deadpanned.

I rubbed at my arms and turned away.

The three guys continued to argue, and I just stared at the far wall, numbers rattling in my head as I considered the possibilities. Like Alcatraz, this prison had never been broken into or out of. Which meant Wild's chances were slim to none.

But were they? She'd smashed the odds before. Mostly because she hadn't been raised in this world, so she didn't see anything as impossible. She didn't know the rules, so she ended up blasting through them.

But I was concerned that she'd opened the connection to us. Had she been forced to? Or had she killed the Shadowkiller so it was safe to do so?

I closed my eyes and reached for that connection between us. She was there, worried but not hurt. Not dying. And she was a little closer than before.

A hand linked with mine, and I held on to Pete, grateful for his solid warmth. "What do you think, Wally? What do we do? You know, you're pretty much her second, right?"

I wasn't sure he was right about that at all. Then again, I'd been able to feel each of the guys in ways they couldn't seem to sense each other.

I turned to look at the three of them. "She's coming for us. I'm sure of it. But I don't . . . I don't have any sort of basis to judge our odds or hers. I don't know what she's up against in the prison here, what kind of traps she could face. I don't know how many people Frost has helping her. I don't know anything. That makes it hard to calculate odds."

A gong sounded through the prison and the

depth of the sound shook me all the way to my bones, rattling inside my chest.

I closed my eyes, and my magic rose around me in an instant to protect me, only to be doused as if I'd been dunked into an ice bath. I gasped, my eyes flying open. I dared to reach for my magic again, and the result was the same. Nothing.

Shivering, I wrapped one arm around my body. "I'm blocked. I can't even feel the dead in here."

Gregory lifted a hand and then stumbled backward, his skin paling. "Me either. Damn, that's cold."

I let go of Pete to rub my arms. I turned my back to them to stare at the wall again. Not because it was so amazing, but because I couldn't figure out how it had been made. Something had been woven through the natural material to create the wall, but who in the five houses had this kind of connection with earth and stone? "Gregory," I said, "what was it you and Professor Ash were doing back in the House of Wonder? Didn't you both use a connection to the earth . . ." I trailed off as I turned.

The boys were gone.

And I was all alone in a box of smooth walls without even a door to bang on. I backed up and leaned against the wall, sliding down until my butt was on the floor.

A wash of fatigue rolled upward from the soles of my feet to the top of my head, where the magic that had wrapped around me tingled.

My strength was being pulled from me, just like Frost had done to the other kids during the Culling Trials.

Which meant we were on a countdown until death came for each of us.

I slumped to the side until I was lying on the floor, not attempting to fight it, conserving my energy, even as I reached for Wild through the connection.

"Come on, Wild. The chances are stupid, the odds are broken. We need your brand of wild magic more than ever before."

My last thought as my strength was sucked away from me was simple and held every hope in my heart.

We needed her to save us.

13

WILD

I stared at the Shadowkiller, my uncle Nicholas, though I had a hard time thinking of the tall asshole as family. Behind us was the rubble of the House of Shade. Or, if Ash was right, the House of Shadows at one point. I wasn't going to waste any time lamenting the fact that it had been destroyed, or that people had died there, or even that I was in seriously deep shit.

"How do I know you're going to hold to your end of the deal?" I said as my feet touched the ground.

His smile was immediate. "Well, that's very easy. You don't. I mean, I wouldn't trust another Chameleon, certainly not one like me. But you don't have much of a choice, now, do you? And so, we go on, and that is how this will be."

What the hell was I supposed to say to that little confession? It lined up with what Gordy had said—that all Chameleons were banana-pants crazy. But why? Was it the power? The kind of magic?

"What drove you crazy?" I asked the question before I thought better of it.

Nicholas shrugged and then smiled again, which he promptly followed up with a wink. "That's easy, I know *exactly* what, but the story is long, and I do believe that your friends are in great danger. Correct? Frost is feeding off them. Drinking deeply as her vampire taught her to do when stealing someone else's life. They have hours, at best, probably less."

"Frost has put them in the prison." I bit the words out. "Ruby helped her, so did Helix."

The father, and maybe the son.

Ash stretched his wings. "The Helix family has deeper ties to all of this than any of us realized. Before this is over, all secrets will be outed, all confessions made. All judgments passed."

Nicholas nodded and turned to take in the debris that had been an academy at one point.

"The houses are intrinsically twined together, but those at the top wish to be separate, and that creates a dissonance felt throughout our world."

I arched a brow at Ash, who gave the slightest of shrugs.

"You mean there's a disturbance in the force?" I offered.

Nicholas laughed softly and brushed a hand across his jaw. "Something like that. An imbalance. A bending of magic that was never meant to be. It has created . . . problems. The servants. The power structure. The houses no longer working together. The sickness affecting our world."

"You mean problems like crazy-ass Chameleons?" I shook my head. "Look, none of this matters right now. What matters is my friends are stuck in that damn prison with Frost. The deal is you will help me get them out, so how about we get on that, okay?"

Nicholas did turn and look at me then. "What makes you think she ever made it to the prison? Because someone *said* she was taken there?"

My heart sank, even though I knew truth when I heard it. "Seriously? They couldn't even get her into a damn prison cell? She was all tied up by the Sandman himself!"

"She has been—for some time—working with the House of Wonder."

Nicholas went on. "They are tied to her through Helix and Daniella. Both of whom are incidentally two of the pets she draws off. I believe Helix was to offer up his son as the next in line." Nicholas held up his hand and little bursts of blue light danced over his fingertips as he flicked them out one at a time. "One, to one, to one. They are all connected. But I cannot see all the threads that bind them, and it's frustrating. Perhaps I should just wipe the rest of that house out."

Holy shit. Holy damn horse shit. My brain was on fire with the implications. Of Ethan being on our crew. Of him being attacked and dying at the end of the Culling Trials. Had that been a test of me and my crew, or had it been something deeper? Had it been punishment for Mr. Helix for not doing something he should have, like handing his son over? A shudder worked its way through me. In the Culling Trials, there hadn't been time for politics, only basic survival. Now . . .

"I see on your face you understand at least some of the implications," Ash said. "It is why, despite his methods, I stay with Nicholas. He may be the most dangerous Chameleon our world has seen, but in his own way, he is trying to better this place. As I can see you are too."

"He killed a whole bunch of people. For no reason. Not self-defense. Not a battle or a war. Just because he could." I pointed at my uncle. Damn, I still didn't like the idea that we were related. Even though it was fairly obvious based on his appearance. I was doing my best not to think about the whole Chameleon connection. I did not need to add 'going crazy' to my growing list of problems.

"Of course, I had reason." Nicholas drew himself up. "They were working for Frost and they were doing things they should not have. The Ice Queen, I sometimes call her if I want to irritate her, was working hard even when I was in the academy to start her rise to the top." And damn it if his eyes didn't sparkle like Tommy's used to whenever he was about to do something he shouldn't.

Nope, nope. I would not get attached to this man who'd been merciless in killing.

A little voice whispered to me. *Any different than the Sandman?*

I frowned. "Look, we're wasting time. I have maps of the prison. I need to get my friends out. If you're really going to stick to this deal, then let's move on it."

"What about the sickness in the House of Wonder?" Nicholas said more to himself, his fingers brushing across his lips. "I have yet to figure out who has created *that* little prezzie. Not Frost. That makes no sense, as it is attacking those she is using. And yet, there is magic in the sickness that grows with each day. So, the question of the day is who pulled the trigger? And how did they get it to focus first on the House of Wonder after the nulls?"

I lowered my bag to the ground, keeping my eyes on him as I took out the map and showed it to Ash. "Not that I don't care, but that's not my priority right now. I've got to get my friends out of that prison before Frost hurts them. After that, we can discuss who is making the House of Wonder sick, why, and how to stop it."

"Not even the Helix boy?" Nicholas glanced over his shoulder. "I thought he was a favorite of yours."

An image of Rory lying still, covered in blood, filled my mind, and I had to fight to push it away. "No. Boys are trouble. Nothing but heartache and stupid ideas. And Ethan apparently killed a friend of mine. So he is on the shit list."

My uncle laughed as if to himself. "I always

thought that too about boys. I tried to tell Lexi that. Not that she listened to me at that age."

"Don't talk about her," I said as I put my bag back on and moved to stand next to Ash. Not that he was my favorite person but . . . if I had to choose which one of these two to be physically closer to, it was Ash, hands down.

Because with Nicholas standing quietly, and not even facing me, there was a steady, low thrum of warning tingling through my body. I wasn't going to ignore it.

"I loved her," he said. "She was my favorite sister."

I tensed and stared hard at him. "I don't care. She was *my* mother, and I don't want you talking about her. Let's focus on the task at hand. How's about that, Tex?"

Yup, just gave the Shadowkiller a nickname.

He smiled at me. "Tex. I'll take that."

And he liked it. Hell, if I didn't know better, I'd say he liked me.

My world had officially turned upside down.

Ash flicked the papers in my hand. "This gives us an idea of where to start. See here? There are several guard towers, more than anywhere else. But I believe it would be the best place to enter."

"That seems counterproductive." I flipped through the pages and saw what was behind the two guard towers: the main cell block. "But the quickest way to get where we need to go?"

Ash nodded. "I do believe we could take them out—"

Nicholas grabbed the map and turned it around. "This? This isn't a map. It's a death trap. Don't even look at it." He snapped his fingers and the flames that had danced across his palm and fingertips ate at the map.

"Son of a bitch!" I drove a fist into his belly, sending him flying backward as I grabbed the map and doused the flames against my chest. "Donkey ass!" I yelled as I patted the papers, the heat sinking through and making me grimace. My hands were still sore from the beating they'd taken from tearing those shadows away from Rory. Pulling the papers off my shirt, I saw the scorch marks were heavy and had eaten most of the papers. Not all of them, but most.

I glared at Nicholas who stood a few feet away, rubbing his belly where I'd socked him. But he didn't retaliate. Shockingly. "You have a hard punch. You know that every Chameleon has a first house? The one they would reside in had they not gained all the abilities?"

"This is not study hall!" I yelled at him. "My friends are in danger, and you promised to help me get them out alive, so we are doing that now! Pull your head out of your butt and let's put a plan together!"

Ash put a hand on my shoulder, and I shrugged him off. "While it may seem roundabout to you, there is often a method to his madness that I've seen more times than I care to admit."

Nicholas was still frowning, rubbing at his body. "I would have been in the House of Night. A first for our family seeing as we come from a long line of Shades."

"I don't—"

"Frost would have been in the House of Wonder. It is her greatest strength." He shrugged and then smiled. "But maybe after I die, I'll come back as a vampire Chameleon."

Horrifying didn't begin to cover that thought.

I looked at Ash. "He wasn't like this before?" Even when he'd first taken me out of the House of Wonder, he'd been more . . . together. Now he seemed to just be following his train of thought wherever it went.

The gargoyle sighed. "He is . . . slipping. He has moments where he is fully the man I know, but in truth, he is slowly losing himself to the power running through him. I don't know if it can be helped. That is why we need you. Or one of the reasons we need you."

Slipping. Like cogs and wheels no longer working together.

"What happens if he *slips* completely?" I asked.

Ash blew out a soft sigh. "Then we will all be in very, very, big trouble." He took me by the arm and led me a few steps away, but Nicholas didn't seem to care. He was staring at what remained of the House of Shade. Ash lowered his voice. "If he loses himself again, then there will be no saving any of us."

Again. That was not any more reassuring than the word *slipping*. "That's what happened the first time, isn't it? When he killed everyone when he was still in the academy."

The gargoyle's dark eyes closed. "Yes. He lost control the first time his abilities converged. He'd been in one of the monthly games, and a friend of his was injured badly. He didn't have a crew like you, or even Frost. He chose to try and keep his magic hidden, to keep it from causing grief. And when it was unleashed, born from fear for his friend, it was unstoppable. He himself wasn't strong enough to control it. Fear will do that."

There was a piece to this I didn't understand.

"How is he so strong without a crew? Without drawing off others? I thought those were the only two ways a Chameleon draws power." I frowned. We had to get moving, but it felt important for me to know this. Both so I could understand Ol' Tex and because I needed to avoid becoming like him. Maybe a little study hall wasn't such a bad thing after all.

Ash gave a low rumble and then shrugged. "That is the crux of it. I don't truly know. I'm not sure if even Nicholas knows."

An uncle with more power than he could handle, and no apparent off switch.

Awesome. Just what I needed.

14

I made my way across the open pier, the sky still dark and littered with clouds that deepened the darkness of the New York waterfront. Pulling out my binoculars, I peered across the water. There was indeed an island in the open ocean, one that I was sure I'd never seen on a map before. And while geography wasn't a strong suit of mine in school, I was sure I'd remember a Shadowspell Island in the New York City harbor.

The walls of the prison were black, and while I could just make them out with the binoculars, I couldn't see much else.

"There is a thick glamor over it," Ash said. "Keeping it hidden from human eyes. And amazingly keeping boats from crashing into it."

"We have to get across the water without them knowing we're coming. Can you carry us both?" I lowered the binoculars and did a quick check over my shoulder at the two men.

Ash shook his head. "I can only carry one at a time."

My uncle spoke up.

"*Them*? Which *them*? These ones or the ones on the other side? Both would kill me if they could, you know?" Nicholas came to stand next to me. That same warning tripped through me, but it was quieter now. Was I getting used to him, like I'd gotten used to Orin? Or maybe I'd realized a deeper truth about him.

He was giving me a glimpse of what my future could be if I wasn't careful. Gah, I did not like the sound of that. Better to focus on the current issue. One problem at a time, no need to go borrowing trouble, as my dad would have said.

"*Them* as in Frost and her crew. Ruby, Helix, whoever else she has there. Whoever they have guarding my friends," I said. "Regular guards, too, I would guess."

"If I fly Nicholas in, the warnings will trip," Ash said, his voice gravelly and smooth at the same time. "It would be best if we arrive at the same time. Nicholas and I can keep the attention of the guards while you get your friends out."

Which meant I needed a ride into that black place. I lifted the binoculars again, staring out at the prison, at the birds that flew in between us. What I wouldn't give for a set of wings right then. But none of the shifters I knew were of the avian variety.

"We should try to hit the prison before the sun is up," Nicholas said, his voice . . . more like before. I looked at him.

"What's this? The good Nicholas?"

His smile was tired. "The sane side of me. I am here less and less. We need to get your friends out so you can come with me. You are the key to our world's problems. Whether you like it or not. That is part of the issue with Frost. She knows that given the right set of tools, you could put her out of business."

"Fabulous. Just what I wanted for my birthday this year," I said, not bothering to hide the sarcasm.

"You aren't afraid of me any longer?" He seemed surprised. Damn, he was right. I wasn't afraid of him anymore. Or at least not petrified. Then again, he also wasn't trying to tie me in knots and kidnap me like he had in the House of Wonder.

"Not like before." I sighed as I tried to figure out just how in the devil's britches I was going to get out to that prison. "Ask me later. The fear status might change."

The Sandman could help maybe? No, I couldn't call on him for this. No doubt, people were watching him now. Frost's spies would know once he brought Rory back.

But the director from the House of Claw, he'd been with the Sandman. The same director who owed me and my crew a favor for our performance in the House of Claw challenge in the Culling Trials. "I've got an idea. It could be a long shot but . . ."

I pulled the walkie-talkie out and flicked it on, scrolling until I found the station the Sandman had been busy yelling at me over. I pressed the button. "You there, Sunshine?"

There was static and white noise for a moment and then, "Wild."

"Rory okay?" I asked.

"He has a good chance," the Sandman growled through the radio.

Sweet relief flowed through me. *A good chance*

was better than a kick in the ass any day. "I need to speak to the director of the House of Claw. He owes me a favor. And I assume since he was with you, he's about as safe as I am going to get when it comes to help."

There was a long stretch of the white static silence. Either the Sandman was ignoring me or he was going to get the director.

"Brutus here," an impossibly deep voice rumbled over the radio.

"I want to cash in that favor," I said. "I need a ride for me and my friends."

He rumbled a deep laugh. "They won't come to you." Yeah, he knew exactly who and what I was hoping to get help from. "Not in the human world. They don't do that for nobody."

"Then I will owe them a little something if they do, and I am good for my word," I said. "Amalthea will come at the very least. I'm sure of it."

In the Culling Trials we'd passed the last test from the House of Claw in nothing short of a spectacular fashion, riding the winged unicorns—alicorns—to our victory. It had been a heady win and, quite possibly, one of the memories that I would always hold on my top ten list. Maybe even top five.

Okay, top two.

A grunt. "You think I keep alicorns inside New York City? You think I could even get them to you before next week?"

"Try," I said. "At least ask them. I'm . . . I'm at Pier 36," I dared to tell him, seeing as we'd be gone in a short matter of time.

Brutus grunted again. "I will ask her. If I can find her."

The line went to static again.

"Someone is coming." Ash tugged on me, and I let him lead me away from the edge of the pier. Nicholas followed more slowly. Of course, he wasn't particularly worried, seeing as he'd just kill anyone in his way.

I reached out and grabbed the edge of his trench coat and bodily dragged him closer to the rubble. "You could pretend to hide at least," I threw at him.

Nicholas raised an eyebrow at me. "Niece, he is not here for me. But you."

He.

My radio squawked, and I turned it down, but too late. The figure in the dark coat, jeans, and ballcap turned our way.

"Rory." I breathed his name, kind of hating

myself for the way it sounded in my ears. Like a girl hankering for her guy. Damn it. But it couldn't be him, he was with the Sandman.

"Wild?"

I had to take another look because I did know him, but he was no Rory. "Ethan? What the hell are you doing here?"

Behind me, Ash and Nicholas faded into the shadows. Reaching Ethan, I grabbed him by the arm, barely restraining myself from shaking him. "Get out of here." Then I remembered he'd killed Colt and trussed up the rest of our friends for Frost, and my hand tightened.

"I came to help," he said. Stupid, stupid boy.

I let him go and swung a hard uppercut, smashing it into his jaw. He stumbled backward, and I stalked after him.

"Your father is working with Frost! You killed Colt, and if I had the time, I'd return the favor! You got *my friends* taken by Frost!" I yelled at him. "What on God's green earth made you think I'd let you get close to me? What makes you think I won't just cut your balls off right here and throw you in the water to bleed out?"

He tried to take my hand, and I twisted his arm around, yanking it up behind his back, and drove him to the ground. "You forget that I am a hell of a lot meaner than any other girl—and a good number of guys—you've ever dealt with."

A grunt slid out of him, but he gave no other indication he was in pain. "Wild, I took the tracking spells off me. My father can't find me again." He tried to look over his shoulder at me. "I swear it. And I didn't . . . I did kill him, you're right —" a short sob rippled out of him, "but it wasn't my idea. I couldn't stop from doing it. Any more than I could stop him from making me spell our friends."

Fuck me. The problem was that I wanted to believe him. I wanted to believe that he'd come through for us in the end. That he wasn't the asshole he always showed himself as. And I wanted him to come with me into the prison. Not because I trusted him, not really. I needed the extra help going up against whatever waited for me. Nicholas was unstable. Ash was not really all that bloodthirsty from what I could see . . . "How do I know, Ethan? You've lied to us before. You've lied to me before."

He nodded. "I'll . . . let you in my head, Wild."

From behind us came a slow clapping. "Oh, I suggest you do that, niece. Being who he is, if you don't vouch for his loyalty to you, I *will* kill him. He could even now be bringing them all down on us. So, I suggest you move quickly."

Crap on a crippled donkey, this was not helping! Ethan didn't fight me. "Please, Wild. Despite the stupid things I've done and said—and I know I've done them—they're my friends too. And I stole a map from my father that should help." He held up a sheaf of papers that looked like a much more complete version of what I'd had.

"How do I . . . get in his head?" I asked Nicholas. "You know, don't you?"

"Easiest way is to kiss him," Nicholas said, and something about his voice told me the saner version of my uncle had slid away again. I just didn't even have it in me to be surprised anymore.

I let Ethan get to his feet. He had a bit of a shadow across his jaw, and there were still dark circles under his eyes. The pressed-clothes, popular boy from the most powerful family in the world had disappeared. Now, he was just like the rest of us. Scrambling to survive.

"A kiss?"

"Or you can drink his blood. That's always been my preferred method," Nicholas drawled. "House of Night and all that."

I wrinkled my nose. I'd kissed Ethan before; I could do it again. I stepped up to him. He was about an inch shorter than me, maybe less. I swallowed hard. "And when I kiss him?" Because there had to be more to it than just a kiss.

"You open yourself to the connection you have. That should do the trick. Pray he is loyal, Wild. Nicholas is not exaggerating," Ash said. When I looked over my shoulder, he was following Nicholas back to the edge of the pier, their backs to us. As if they were giving us some semblance of privacy.

"You're . . . working with the Shadowkiller?" The shock in Ethan's voice would have been funny under any other circumstance. As it was, this was the least humorous I'd felt in a long, long time.

"Just kiss me, you idiot. I'll explain later, assuming I don't see a reason to just hand you over to him," I grumbled as I pulled him toward me. "And no tongue." Our lips met, and his hands went to my waist. I kept my eyes open and so did he. Like we were twelve years old experiencing our first kiss.

I kind of doubted that a peck on the lips was going to do the trick if blood was the other option.

We were going to have to really kiss to make this connection happen.

Damn it.

Reluctantly, I let my eyes flutter closed and leaned into the kiss, opening my mouth, not thinking about him at all. Thinking about someone with dark hair and eyes. Someone who was fighting for his life.

Once more, I'd surprised Ethan, and I could feel his hesitance for a few seconds before he put one hand to the back of my head and pulled me close.

I couldn't even say it was nice, not when I knew he'd killed Colt. There was nothing in this kiss, not for me—even for this much, I had to pretend he was someone else. But by the feel of Ethan's body, he was enjoying the kiss a hell of a lot more than I was. Inside my head, I found the thin golden threads of my connection to Ethan, and I tapped into them, not sure what to expect.

A bloom of heat started at the bottom of my feet and raced upward, through my legs, belly, and chest, wrapping around my neck and then out of my mouth and into Ethan. He groaned and my hands tightened on him at the same exact moment his tightened on me.

This was some serious magic.

He angled his mouth to take the kiss deeper, and I let him, a whisper of something more there sliding through me. *Maybe there* was *magic between us after all.* As I thought it, the connection between us blazed, like a conduit that had just opened up, and the magic flowed back and forth lazily, touching every part of me. Warming me from the inside out, soothing away some of the exhaustion, some of the aches and pains. I hiked a leg up over his hip, and he let out a low groan as he pulled me closer, grinding against me.

For me, it wasn't that I desired him. Not in that way. I wanted to *absorb* him. And that freaked me the hell out but I couldn't stop myself.

I wrapped my arms around him as if I could climb inside of him and understand what went on inside of his head. Closer, I needed to be closer.

That need for connection, for joining to another soul flared out around me, and I couldn't help but reach out to my other friends.

They were not far, but they felt like they were on the other side of the world. And there was no response from them . . . either they were sleeping or unable to reach back to me.

Concerning.

And then I was pulled deep into Ethan, inside his head in a way I hadn't thought possible. His most recent memory exploded inside my mind, like light responding to a flicked switch. I saw it as if I were an observer, rather than through Ethan's eyes.

"You are my son! And you will serve who I tell you to serve!" Mr. Helix held his wand at the ready, as if threatening to use it on Ethan.

Half slumped against the wall, Ethan had clearly been fighting his father for some time. He had an open wound on his face, and his left eye was swelling shut. "I won't let you tell me who I can care about anymore. You . . . how could you force that on me? If you wanted him dead, you could have done it yourself! Why did you make me kill him . . ." A sob tore out of Ethan, his body shaking. "And now you want me to turn on Wild too? Wasn't it enough that you made me turn on my friends?"

Helix laughed. "They do not think of you as a friend, Ethan."

He glared at his father, his face wet. "I won't do it."

"Colt was strong enough that he could have become a problem. Not to mention, he had Ruby in his sights. Your job is and always will be to protect Frost and her people. Ruby is one of her people. I am one of her

people. And soon you will be too." Mr. Helix stalked across the room, pulling out an object I recognized. The sunburst medallion the House of Wonder kids had all worn. "Now, the girl is special. You're right about that. I didn't realize . . . or I would have done something about her sooner."

My mind flickered back to Colt's death. The blast of magic. Ethan's stricken face as he stood over his friend. My belly felt as though it had been filled with rocks, sinking to the floor. He'd been under a compulsion spell even then. And I thought I had it bad with my uncle being the Shadowkiller.

"You will find the young Chameleon, and you will bring her back to me," Mr. Helix said as he approached his son.

Shit, shit! Helix knew what I was? But, of course, if he was with Frost. She'd told him. Which meant my secret was well and truly out.

Ethan shuddered. "Why? What do you want to do to her?"

"She is the key to this world. She just doesn't know it. And I will be the one to hold her leash."

Oh, shit, that did not sound good.

"No! I won't do it. I won't be what you *want anymore!" Ethan roared, and pointed his wand, not at*

his father, but at his own left shoulder. A flash of light and then nothing.

The scene went completely dark. I could have dug in farther, but I could feel the pain vibrating off Ethan from just that single memory. We weren't actively kissing anymore but standing close with our foreheads touching. The connection between us was running hot, his magic sliding under my skin with a pleasant buzzing sensation.

This was what it was like to kiss someone in your crew, and suddenly I could see the draw of it, could see why Frost had been with her vampire lover. What if I had been in love with Ethan? How much stronger would this have been between us?

This was why Jared had stayed with Frost even while she aged. This was . . . *addictive* was the only word I had for it.

I wondered what he felt, and the second I questioned it, I knew. He felt safe, here with me. Despite the situation, Ethan felt safe. For the first time in a long time, despite the Shadowkiller being so very close.

I blinked and looked into his eyes. "He made you kill Colt."

Ethan groaned. "I . . . I couldn't stop it. I wanted to, but I didn't realize what was going on until it was too late. I couldn't let him do the same to you and the others... that's why I did what I did. I can't lose you too, Wild. I know I've been an ass. I'll probably still be an ass after all this is done, but I'm here. I'm with you. All the way."

I bit the inside of my cheek, a part of me still wanting to hate him, but I couldn't. Being controlled like that by his own father? "Are you sure you're free of him?"

"My left shoulder was where the bindings he had on me were buried. Deep in my shoulder." It was then that I realized he'd barely lifted that hand. "It'll get better."

I was not a hugs-and-kisses kind of girl, so I think it surprised me as much as him when I pulled him in for a tight hug. "I've got your back, Ethan. Even if you are a dick some days."

He hesitated and then hugged me, though that left side was weaker for sure. "I've got yours too, Johnson. Even though you're a boss bitch and I'm . . . beginning to doubt you need me." His smile slipped. "Not an easy thing for a Helix to say."

He pulled back from me first. "What do we do now? The prison is out in the harbor. They'd see boats coming a literal mile away."

I nodded. "I know. I'm hoping to cash in on a favor."

Ethan frowned. "What kind of favor?"

I smiled, and it widened at the sound of wings whooshing through the air. "The kind that involves a kick-ass ride."

15

I'd hoped for one alicorn—Amalthea, the boss mare I'd ridden in the trials—but I got all of them. Okay, not all of them, but the alicorns that each of my crew had ridden to our victory.

Amalthea was as stunningly beautiful as the first time I'd seen her, maybe more so in the dark of night, the city lights in the background giving her coat a silvery cast. Was it weird seeing a creature like her here in New York City, so out of place? You bet. But weird was pretty much the name of the game in my life now, and I didn't even blink.

Time to roll with things and rescue my friends.

After a quick hello to the alicorns, I grabbed hold of Amalthea's mane and leapt onto her back, making sure not to hit her wings. “We need to get to that rock out there—” I pointed out to the island, “—and then can you wait for us? We’ll need a ride back.”

The mare bobbed her head, horn sparkling impossibly bright. Glowing on its own like a beacon.

I turned to see Ash standing next to Nicholas. “We will meet you on the southern side. There is a narrow strip of beach there where the alicorns can land. I do not believe they will trip any alarms.”

Tightening my legs around Amalthea’s barrel, I nodded. “See you on the other side.”

Ash blinked. “Perhaps a different saying would be best, considering what we are headed into.”

He wrapped his arms around Nicholas and launched into the air with a powerful leap. One flap of his wings, and he was high above us, soaring toward the prison.

“You sure you can trust them?” Ethan asked from atop another alicorn.

I shook my head. “Not at all. But to get the others out, I’d sell my soul to the devil himself.”

Ethan’s blue eyes were sharp. “You may have done just that.”

“I know.”

Shit, did I ever know, and Ethan didn't even know the half of it. That I'd agreed to go with Nicholas after my friends were safe.

"Ethan," I said, looking away from him, "no matter what happens, promise me you'll get them all out."

His voice was hard. "What aren't you telling me?"

I didn't answer him. Mostly because I wasn't sure why I was holding back. He should know what I'd given Nicholas in return for his help.

But I couldn't bring myself to tell him. I urged Amalthea forward and she took off at a gallop, her unshod hooves thudding dully across the wooden pier as she stretched out her wings and picked up speed. At the end of the pier, she leapt up, her wings taking us high in a matter of seconds.

The wind whipped around me, cold and damp, and although the alicorns were no less spectacular now than they'd been during the trials, it was nowhere near the same sensation. Back then, I'd felt free, without a care in the world.

Now . . . I was riding into a trap. One I'd agreed to. "Do I have to keep my word to them?" I whispered into the wind.

I was a Shade, through and through, and what was our motto? Survival. At all costs.

A solid sense of understanding slid through me. Whatever the cost, I would survive this, and so would my friends.

Ethan and his mount flew closer and the other alicorns followed behind us at a distance. "Do you have a plan?" he shouted over the wind.

"I think we go in the south end and deal with whatever comes our way. I can find them." I tapped my head. "We just have to get close enough for me to pinpoint their location."

The air seemed to get colder the closer we got to the prison. Shadowspell Island Penitentiary rose up ahead of us, a black, blocky building as imposing as its name. The alicorns swept around to the south side with little urging from me, and they came in across the shallow water for landing.

Amalthea's hooves caught the very edge of the waves as we dropped, sending up a cold, salty spray of water before she hit the sand and immediately slowed to a smooth trot, tossing her head and flipping her mane back and forth. The strip of beach was only about ten feet from water to the rocks that went straight up to the base of the prison, but it was long, about a mile and a half by the looks of it.

We approached the two figures waiting for us, and a whisper of a warning hissed through me. Ethan and his mount and the other alicorns landed behind us, letting us lead the way.

Ash and Nicholas didn't move but instead waited for us to approach. I slid off Amalthea's back and whispered softly to her, "Be ready to leave. If someone spots you, get your ass out of here. Don't wait for us if it isn't safe."

She bobbed her head, flashing her horn in a way that made me think anyone who came to bother them would be in for a pointed response.

I patted her neck, then started toward the other pair. Ethan dismounted and grabbed my arm. "Wait. I have something for you. I snagged it from my dad's office when he wasn't looking."

He slid something cylindrical and smooth into my hand, and I stared down at my wand. "How?"

"I have no idea. I'm thinking you dropped it in the House of Wonder, and he found it." He shrugged. "That's my guess."

I tucked the wand into one of the knife sheaths strapped to my legs. A tight fit but at least it would do. "Thanks."

He reached out as if to touch me, but his hand dropped before he made contact. “I trust you, Wild. But I don’t trust them.” His head tipped toward Ash and Nicholas.

“You and me both.”

When we were close enough that we didn’t have to yell, Ash motioned for us to hurry up. “There is not much time before the guards sweep this area. They check it every hour or so. From what we can tell, we’ve not yet tripped the alarms. This is good.”

Nicholas said nothing, motioning for me to go ahead of him.

“Yeah, no. You go first, Ethan behind you, and I’ll bring up the rear.”

My uncle smiled, soft and sad, but said nothing.

Ash climbed the rocks that led up to the base of the prison walls like they were nothing, his fingers and toes tipped in sharply pointed claws that allowed him amazing purchase. Or maybe it was his connection to the earth. Nicholas followed him fairly easily, as did Ethan.

The sheer rock was straight up, but broken and jagged so somewhat perfect for climbing. It looked as though it turned into a thin ledge at the top, at the base of the prison walls.

My mind was a million miles away as I followed them. I knew it wasn't smart to be distracted when I was trying to sneak up a sheer wall of rock on a cold, wet, dark night.

But my thoughts kept circling back to things I just didn't understand.

Namely that my uncle hadn't made the House of Wonder fall sick. But then who had? And who was truly helping Frost? What if we didn't stop her? Did she get to be like a queen or something?

The words of Gordy the goblin whispered through me: "One of them has to win. We just got to keep them both from taking over."

Was that a possibility?

My mouth dried up and my throat tightened. "Ethan, did your dad say what," I paused and realized that I didn't want to say anything in front of Ash or Nicholas. Yes, they were waging a fight against Frost too, but . . . something held me back from speaking. And I wanted to know what exactly Frost might be looking for.

Ethan looked over his shoulder at me, his left hand gripping at a rock. "What?"

Fate intervened.

Ethan's left hand spasmed, releasing his hold on the slick rocks. He windmilled hard, falling back straight toward me.

I slid to the side, digging my right hand into a crevice as I shot my left hand out to grab at him as he fell. My fingers tangled in the side of his shirt and his weight—damn him and his muscle building—pulled me hard, swinging us both out into open space with just my one hand holding us up.

"Damn it!" I growled, wishing I could shout. Or had wings.

The connection between me and my friends broke open wide, and I clung to Gregory's connection to . . . stone. My fingers clenched harder, and it was as if my palms had become sticky to the surface of the rock like Velcro. The slide stopped and I hung there.

"Ethan, can you reach the rock?"

He answered by grunting and twisting around while still dangling from my hold. I had to close my eyes and breathe through the burn of my muscles reminding me that he was hardly Gregory or Wally. Ethan was all muscle and solid as they came.

"Hurry."

"I'm trying, don't rush me."

A stupid grimace that was almost a smile rolled over my face. "That's what he said."

From above us, one of the men snickered. I'd bet any money I had left it was my uncle. Tommy would have laughed at the joke too.

Ethan managed to get his hands back on the rock and slowly made his way up next to me. "Thanks."

I stared at him, not sure what to think of this new Ethan. I'd been in his head; I'd felt his sincerity and how tangled up his emotions were when it came to me. But I almost missed the snarky, too-confident playboy from the beginning of the Culling Trials.

"Why are you staring at me? We should be climbing. Or did you change your mind?" he said as he pulled himself up with a grimace.

"Just thinking about how much you've changed," I said as I matched him in speed and made sure not to let him get too far ahead of me. If he slipped again, I needed to be close. I, on the other hand, wasn't going anywhere—in the slipping sense. My borrowed Gregory power was still in full force, my hands adhering to the rock as if I were wearing sticky gloves.

"I didn't have a choice," Ethan said softly. "Either I changed and came with you, or I turned into my father and ended up just like him, tied to Frost."

Something in me turned over, ugly and dark. "So, you had to choose between Chameleons."

"That's about the whole of it," he said, not looking at me.

He had to pick which Chameleon he belonged to, and while he'd chosen me, I didn't like that he'd had to choose at all.

"I'll let you go when this is all done, Ethan," I said. "You won't have to be with any Chameleon."

He shot me a look and opened his mouth, but we'd reached the top. Ash and Nicholas waited and there was no chance for Ethan to speak. The building shot straight up in front of us, high above our heads, easily four stories above ground just like the schematics had shown. The rocks we'd climbed flattened out at the top, but the lip they stood on was barely a foot wide, less in places.

Ash's skin blended into the stone until he was barely visible. "The guard is changing now, hurry."

And he all but pushed us forward, before Ethan and I were even all the way onto the narrow ledge. Ethan shot me a look, and I nodded.

Yeah, I didn't like it either.

Not for one second.

But there was really no choice. I was in front, and with my back to the wall, I kept my one arm flat against the prison, still using my connection to Gregory to keep my purchase solid.

At the corner of the building, I peeked around and saw a wider platform leading to a main door that, while it wasn't big, was guarded.

And not by just anyone.

No. No, my luck was not that good.

Ruby stood with her arms crossed over her chest and a smile on her lips. "Come out, come out wherever you are, young Chameleon." She drew in a deep breath. "I can smell your fear."

16

I looked over my shoulder at Ethan. "You got any cloaking spells?"

"Like what?" he asked.

"Invisibility?"

He snorted.

Hey, a girl could dream.

"I can pull shadows around myself—"

Nicholas held up a hand. "You need to face her. She knows we are coming. Might even know we are here."

I stared at him. "She whooped my ass—soundly, I'm going to say—the last time I met her."

"The last time you met her, you were spelled to dull your abilities. And she didn't whoop you—she couldn't kill you no matter how hard she tried. You aren't dulled now, Maribel." Eyes as blue as my own stared hard into me. "You can take her."

A slow string of curses slid out of me. If Ruby knew I'd been dulled—assuming my uncle was right—she wouldn't wait for me to hit solid ground to face her. She'd kill me while I tried to creep my way around the side of the building.

I looked down at the rocks below. They swept around and under the platform. "I've got an idea. Ethan, as soon as I have her distracted, you go for the door."

"On it." He pulled his wand clear.

Taking a deep breath, I crouched, using my sticky fingers to creep low, below her line of vision, and went around the corner of the building. Working my way across the rocks, I moved slowly, keeping my eyes on her and letting my body *feel* its way over the slick surfaces.

When I was just under the platform, I paused to catch my breath and slow my heart.

"She won't come this way, Frost," Ruby said, and the squawk of a walkie-talkie rippled to me. "She'd be a fool to try to face me. I nearly killed her yesterday."

White static, and then a voice that I would never forget slid over the speaker. "She will want to face you. It is in her nature to prove herself. Just as it was in her mother's. Just as it is in her uncle's. Do not kill her, Ruby. I want her alive."

"And if I must?"

"I will be . . . displeased."

The static flicked back on, and Ruby let out a curse. "Displeased, my ass. That kid is going to die."

So much for being safe because Frost wanted me alive.

I reached up around the edge of the platform, pushing off with my feet and pulling up with my hands at the same time so I launched up and landed on the platform in a crouch.

Ruby did not look surprised.

"Frost is going to be *displeased* if you kill me. I imagine that won't be pleasant," I said as I pulled both knives from their sheaths.

She snorted. "Oh, little girl, you know so little. Let me guess, your uncle brought you here? He thinks you can best me, does he?"

I shrugged as if her words meant nothing. "I came alone. I wouldn't risk anyone else."

Ruby slid her hands over her knife-covered vest, as if picking one by feel. She stopped on two blades that were all too familiar to me. The two coated in different poisons.

Damn. So not only did I need to beat her, I needed to keep her from even nicking me with an edge or tip. There were no healers here to help me.

"You think you can beat me this time?" She stepped to the side. "I don't think you have any idea what you're up against. And no Sandman to rescue you."

"I guess we're about to find out." I feinted to the left. She followed, and when I came back with a strike, she blocked my thrust with her own knife. The weapons clanged off one another, and I used the momentum to swing my second knife, slashing it across her chest.

The tip of my knife caught on something in her vest, and she jerked sideways, taking my blade with her.

"Too young to know better." She laughed as she turned back to me, the blade still sticking out. Ruby reached up and tugged the handle. "You don't think Frost would actually let me go into a fight with just a leather vest, do you?"

As she held the knife out, the blade slowly disintegrated, falling into dust until there was nothing left in her hand. She'd let me hit her, knowing what would happen.

Crap on a cactus, this would be far worse than I'd thought.

I stepped back, drawing her with me. If nothing else, I had to clear the path for Ethan to get into the prison.

Our blades clashed again, and I stepped back once more, making space for Ethan, Ash, and Nicholas. Clash and step, clash and step. I ducked a swing of her fist, drove a blow of my own toward her middle but she wasn't there.

I couldn't tell if I was faster, or if she was playing with me. Either way, I'd put at least fifteen feet between her and the door. That had to be enough for the guys to get through. Didn't it?

Of course, it was only then that I considered the fact that Nicholas could have taken Ruby on with very little effort. Yet, here I was—I blocked a wicked fast strike coming straight for my neck—fighting for my life against a woman who had years of training on me.

The best in the business, and I'd only just started my internship.

"I see it in your eyes, you've just realized something." She smiled. "That you're going to die?"

"That I might be being played," I gritted out. I reached for the connection I had with Ethan, not to draw on him. But to get him ready.

In case I couldn't do this on my own. Weirdly, Frost was right. I needed this moment to prove myself to me, not to anyone else.

Her laugh rang across the space between us. "Oh, little girl, that's a given in this world. If you aren't at the top, you're being shit on and used. Why do you think I took up with Frost? I was tired of being pushed around."

I sidestepped a fist and kicked out, catching her in the hip with the point of my boot, just like the Sandman had done to me. She snarled and had to step back. Damn, that was not what I wanted.

Very carefully, I lowered my hands a little, feigning fatigue.

Come on, follow me, you malevolent little redhead.

I blinked and Ruby was there within my guard, her black-bladed knife coming straight for my face. I dropped to one knee and slashed my remaining blade across her inner thigh, right down to the bone.

She shrieked, and I rolled as she swept her knives at my back. My heartbeat didn't speed up as

I stood—it actually slowed, flowing calm energy through me.

Spinning my blade in my hand, I met her suddenly frantic slashes, her eyes wide. "You are not faster than me. You are not better than me!"

I caught each blow aimed at me and matched it, slammed a fist into her jaw and rocked her back on her heels. She tried to use my own trick on me, going to her knees and slashing at my inner thigh, but I dove out of the way, putting my back to the main doors and maneuvering Ruby closer to the edge of the overhang.

I stood and stared at her. I knew as she did there was no mercy given in this fight, no tying up your opponent and hoping they changed their mind to become a better person. It was kill or be killed.

No mercy.

No remorse.

She stayed on her knees, swaying. It was only then I saw the number of slashes across her body, her face and legs. I'd managed to avoid the vest covered in the metal-eating spell. Anywhere skin showed—and a few places it didn't—she was slick with blood.

"You won't find them." She smiled. "Not even

with me gone, you won't get them out. That's not how this is going to end, little girl. No one wins in this world. Certainly you won't be any different."

"I guess you'll never know," I said.

She looked over her shoulder. "I'll make it easy on you." Without another word, she threw herself backward, over the edge of the platform. One second there, the next gone.

A footstep sounded behind me. Ethan's energy touched me first and then his hand on my arm. "You okay? Did she hit you with her blades?"

"Not this time," I said, unable to take my eyes from the place she'd been just a moment before. I made myself walk forward and look over the edge. The black of the rocks and the water far below didn't show me anything. She was gone, but I'd have bet my last knife she wasn't dead.

17

You know that moment in the horror movie where you know that it's a total and complete setup? That moment you're yelling at the screen for the characters to run away? Yeah, get ready for it.

I stepped forward, eyes on the door while I motioned for the others to follow me. I put a hand on the door that led into the massive, stark prison, and it opened with barely a push. It wasn't locked. It wasn't even *shut*. Nor was there a spell on it, or a monster waiting for me. This place was basically an open invitation to said horror show ahead of us.

Just peachy.

"You know, if our friends weren't in here, this would be a terrible idea," I said.

Ethan handed me my backpack, and I pulled my trusty-ish flashlight out before I slid the bag back on.

"It's a terrible idea no matter who is in there," he said.

Holding the light up, I flicked it through the first room, the dim beam landing on solid black walls without a single visible doorway. "No lights? Not very original," I muttered, my voice echoing down the long dark hallway. And then it echoed back to me, distorting into a weird hiccupping laugh that was not my own.

Ethan pressed a little closer to me, and I didn't care that I did the same with him.

If I were to guess, I'd say vampire. I flicked the light upward, unable to see the ceiling or, what would have been worse, a vampire hanging from the ceiling. I did not need a repeat of my old friend Barnaby creepy crawling toward me. The walls seemingly shot straight up the entire four stories without a single thing to break up the monotony of the black stone.

Ethan held up his wand, the tip glowing and giving off a faint light. "You want to hear better news?"

"Shit, why not?" I said.

"Ash and the Shadowkiller slipped away while you were fighting Ruby."

I turned and flicked the light toward the doors behind us. "And here I'd thought they were just being slow."

There was no part of me that wasn't on guard now.

"I really meant it was better," Ethan said as he stepped in time with me, making our way down the hall. "You aren't dumb enough to think he's on our side. Tell me your brains didn't leak out since the Culling Trials."

I didn't so much as look at him, just kept my eyes on the space in front of us. "There you are. I thought I'd lost the *real* you to your emotions. Glad to see I was wrong."

"What?"

"Ash said they'd slip away at some point to distract the guards. Until I see evidence otherwise, I'm going to assume that's what they're doing." I kept my voice low, and even then, it still echoed a little.

I kept scanning the place we were in, looking for the inevitable traps. It wasn't until I looked down at the tiles below our feet that I saw them. I grabbed Ethan, stopping him in his tracks. "Don't move."

He froze and I bent to brush a hand over the slightly raised tile just ahead of him. I'd noticed the way the edge of it reflected as my light swept over it. "Get behind me. I'll lead, you follow. Last thing we need is you setting off a booby trap."

"I do like the view," he said under his breath as I stepped out around the tile and in front of him. "Nice . . . jeans."

"Not the time, Ethan." I moved forward and let myself fully open up to the connection between me and my friends. Gregory was the closest—unsurprising given the way I'd been able to borrow his abilities—so I followed the pull toward him.

That sensation of Gregory in my head took me past several more raised tiles in the floor. I swept the flashlight repeatedly across the checked floor, avoiding stepping on any of them.

Go me.

I stopped against the far right side of the wall and leaned my head up against it. No, that wasn't quite right. I crouched and put my hand on the floor. "They put Gregory in the floor?"

Ethan stood behind me, his back to the wall. "Any idea on how to get him out?"

I snorted. "Any idea why we haven't run into more problems?"

All the questions and no answers.

His swallow was audible. "A trap."

Yeah, that was exactly what I was thinking. "Better that we move quickly, then." I stepped back and pointed at the tile below us. "Can you blast it?"

He blinked. "Seriously?"

"It's not like they don't know we're here, and we're just wasting time by going slow at this point," I said.

Ethan stepped back, and I grabbed hold of him as his heel brushed against one of the many raised tiles. "No better ideas?"

"None that are quick," I said and put my fingers to my ears as he raised his wand.

"*Lavium braken*!" He snapped the words, and I committed them to memory along with the counter-clockwise swirl he did with his wand. The tip of his wand glowed a deeper red, and instead of blasting out as I'd thought it would, the wand dripped magic off in a ruby red fiery droplet. The droplet fell and landed on the tile with a plop.

Hissing and snapping, the magic ate through the tile, spreading outward like a virus eating away at the building itself.

A booming alarm ripped through the air, breaking the silence. I peered down into the hole.

Chains hung from the underside of the floor to at least fifty feet below. Smack in the middle of them, bound hand and foot, was Gregory, his blond head barely visible under all the chains.

Ethan grabbed my arm as I stepped closer to the opening. "Don't touch the edges of the magic. It'll spread on anything it touches until the power recedes. Remember that."

I shrugged out of my backpack. "Wait here. I'll climb down and get him." I handed Ethan my pack. "Kill anything that comes this way, unless it's Ash and Nicholas."

"Who the hell is Nicholas? Is that the Shadowkiller?"

Right, he only knew him as the Shadowkiller. I threw him a grin, knowing this would throw him off. "My uncle." I hopped out into the open space and fell for a beat before I reached out and grabbed one of the chains.

"What the hell?" he shouted after me.

For just a moment I was freefalling, I felt . . . light. Beyond all logic, I felt convinced we were going to get our friends out of there. That we'd get the hell away from the prison and, better yet, away from Frost.

Mind you, there was that little promise I'd made to the Shadowkiller. Uncle Nicholas.

I gritted my teeth as I worked across the chains, swinging to get closer to Gregory.

The buzzing of bees worked its way into my ears, and I slowed, my hands and legs wrapped around one long chain. "What the hell is that?" I said more to myself than to Gregory. But he heard me.

His head jerked up, and I saw his mouth was stuffed with a gag. But a thought came through loud and clear from him, frantic. Intense.

Lightning.

"Lightning?" I said, and that buzzing came again, setting a riot of understanding through my brain.

Not lightning.

Electricity.

Well, shit on my cowboy boots, this was not going to be so simple as I'd hoped. I got the barest warning down my spine and leapt away from the chain I was on to a neighboring one. The one I'd left lit up, buzzing like mad as electricity rumbled down it and I spun in a full circle on my new lifeline.

I scrambled to swing to the next chain, grabbing hold as the metal around me began to light up in intervals. Part of my brain said this was stupidly like the Culling Trials—a game to beat. But there was no pattern to the pulsing electricity, at least not that I could see yet.

The other part said that at some point whoever was pressing the buttons would just hit the "fry them all" lever and the electricity would run through all the chains.

"Hang on, Gregory!" I hollered as I got closer. Not that he couldn't see I was coming, but I could feel his fatigue.

Whatever was being done to him was draining him of energy. And some of it was me borrowing his abilities. Which were helping me even then.

I caught hold of one of the chains he was wrapped in, and slid down it, my fingers burning as I gripped at the last second to stop my freefall.

His head rolled, and I could see he was fully bound in not only ropes that held his wrists and ankles tightly, but a collar made of steel that wrapped loosely around his neck. Anger burst through me like the electricity that danced around us. I yanked my knife free and slashed through the ropes first, then with a hard backswing, drove the knife between the links attached to his collar.

"Hurry," he groaned as the knife stuck against the steel.

"It won't break." I shook my head and then looked upward. The hole was well above us and a long climb no matter how I looked at it. But if I couldn't get Gregory's collar off, it wouldn't matter. Unless . . .

"I'm going to use a spell, but we have to time it just right." I stuffed my knife away and helped Gregory up so we were hanging onto the same chain. I checked the trajectory of the electricity, grabbed the chain next to us, and pulled him with me. The chain we'd been on lit up, went dull again, and I grabbed it, swinging us back. That would buy us some time. Not a lot, but maybe enough.

"Hurry up!" Ethan yelled. "We've got incoming!"

Of course we did.

I pulled my wand out and pointed the tip at the connection between the chain and Gregory's neck. "Soon as it loosens, I'm going to yank it away. We can't let it touch your skin, okay?"

Gregory nodded. "I trust you."

Crap, I wasn't sure I trusted me, not with spells. But it was what we had.

I held the wand tip about six inches up the chain, away from Gregory. "*Lavium braken,*" I said as I did the whole swirl backward thing. The tip of the wand glowed, but it was black, not red. Sweet baby jeebus, why did it have to be black?

"Hang on, this could go really, really bad," I said as the droplet of black hung for a moment off the tip of the wand and then dripped onto the chain.

The metal disintegrated just like with Ethan's spell, and my black spell spread outward—fast. Way faster than Ethan's. It was at Gregory's neck in seconds, and I yanked on either side of the collar hard, shattering the last bit of metal before the rapidly spreading spell could touch his skin. Down it went, into the abyss below us.

I looked up as my black spell raced up the chain, leaving a bit of ashy dust behind.

"Thanks," Gregory grumbled, and then I was dragging him upward as my eyes tracked the patterns of the electricity dancing amongst the chains.

"Why aren't they just killing us?"

I pulled Gregory up, so he was on my back. He clung weakly to me. "You want them to?"

"It's a prison. Not the Culling Trials. Why not just blast us? This doesn't make sense." Sweat made my hands slippery as I fought to climb the chains, my back and legs burning with the exertion. I couldn't take any of his abilities anymore. It would eat into his reserves. Gregory's exhaustion was real, and I did what I could, sending him energy until he patted me on the head. "Enough. I'm awake now."

"Good, I was starting to get tired," I said as I counted the beats of the electricity lighting up the space around us and moved us to the left, swinging onto another chain while our original one lit up again, then grabbed hold of it once it had gone quiet and kept on climbing.

So far, as bad as it was, this prison wasn't as hard as the trials.

I was weirdly disappointed.

And really, that was the moment I knew I needed to have my head examined. Maybe all Chameleons really were crazy. Maybe we all needed a thrill or something? A fix of adrenaline?

I didn't know and didn't really care right then.

Because we were nearly out. I could almost

reach the edge of the hole, but I didn't dare. I didn't know if Ethan's magic had finished doing its thing.

"Ethan?" I hollered up.

"Ethan?" Gregory's hold on me tightened. "What in the name of—"

"You said you trusted me, I'll explain later," I said then hollered again. "Ethan, little help here!"

"Busy!" he yelled, and there was a distinct sound of bootsteps, a grunt, and a thump of a body hitting the ground.

I stared up at the empty space. Gregory's hand's tightened around my shoulders.

"Wild, I think . . ."

I didn't get to hear what he thought because the timing of the electricity changed.

"Gregory, hang on!" I yelled as the electricity arced through the chain I was hanging onto and every other chain around us. Damn, this was a mean end game.

I threw us off, out into mid-air, missing the shocking jolt that I had no doubt would have killed us.

"Wild, you got wings?" Gregory yelped as we fell straight down. Not touching any of the chains.

"Nope!"

We fell, the electricity danced, and I waited.

The seconds felt like eternity and then the electricity finally died.

I reached for the dangling chains, my fingers slipping over them—two fingers snapping—before I finally got a hold on the very bottom of a chain, literally hanging from the bottom links.

We swayed there a minute. "I don't think they'll send any more electricity through."

Gregory's weight pulled on me, and I tried to reach up with my bad hand to pull us farther up but even clenching that hand was nearly impossible. "Shit."

"This is a problem," Gregory said. "You can't climb?"

My last two fingers on my right hand were definitely broken, and I struggled to breathe through the sudden sharp pain now that the moment was wearing off. Who knew such small bones could cause such immense hurt?

"Give me a second. I'll try again," I said as I hung there, breathing hard.

Gregory climbed off my back and up the chain, nimble as ever. He turned upside down so we were kind of face to face. "Wild, we're a team. I'll get help."

And just like that, we might as well have been

back in the Culling Trials. I smiled up at him. "Ethan's at the top—his father made him kill Colt and help Helix take the rest of you. I trust him. But his magic ate through the floor, and if it's still active, that would not be good to touch. Same magic as the one I used to break the chain."

"I trust you, Wild, so for now I'll trust Wonder Bread." And for the life of me, Gregory winked and climbed the chain hand over hand, heading straight up.

Which gave me time to think. I mean, I wasn't about to let go and drop God only knew how far down.

With that in mind, I peered down into the depths below me. Hell, for all I knew the floor was only a few feet below me. Though I doubted it.

I closed my eyes and reached through the connection that tied us together to my friends. Pete was closer than I would have thought. In fact . . . "Wait! Gregory! Tell Ethan to come down here!"

"Are you serious?"

I looked up at him, about halfway up. "I think we can get to Pete this way! Ethan, check the maps!"

"Are you serious?" He repeated himself, and I

twisted around. Pete wasn't far at all. Maybe twenty feet below me.

And that meant that the ground couldn't be that far. Right?

Right. Gregory hollered my question up to Ethan.

There was a pause, and while I couldn't hear paper being rustled I was hoping.

"Yeah, I think the shifters could be below. Shit." Ethan's voice echoed down to us.

"Then, come on!" I hollered up through the empty space. A moment later, a figure was sliding down the chains, moving fast.

Gregory made his way back down to me. "We could have pulled you up. And found a better doorway into the shifters. Rather than dropping through the roof into the pen of some wolf pack."

"As Orin pointed out, I've got a metric ton of muscle on me," I said as I swayed slightly back and forth. "No one wants to lift me anywhere. And we aren't going to drop on a wolf pack."

Hopefully.

Ethan reached us a moment later, his wand held between his teeth, the end lit up like a glowstick.

"You okay?" Whoever he'd been fighting with

up there he'd handled. But that didn't mean he'd not gotten hurt in the scuffle.

He nodded and his eyes met mine and clearly said one thing. *Now what?*

"Now," I loosened my hold on the chains, "we let go."

18

The thing about having a little bit of faith is that it's terrifying when you can't see where you're leaping. Leap before you look, you say. Leap and the ground will appear. Well, this was more of a let go and hope that you weren't killing yourself and your friends.

I only knew that going back up the chains and down that main hall where the echoing laughter had come from was a terrible idea. That was what would be expected of us.

We had to do the unexpected. And maybe, just maybe it would save us all.

The air whooshed around me, and before I knew it, I'd hit solid ground. Ten feet, no more.

That wasn't too bad. At least until the boys dropped off the chains.

Two bodies hit, Gregory landing on top of me, knocking the wind out of me a second time.

Ethan landed to the side of me, at least, and let out a low groan. "I thought we would land on something softer. I thought that was why you let go. Because you could see something."

"I did land on something softer." Gregory rolled off me. "Well, kinda. Wild is not really soft."

I was flat on my back, and I pushed into a sitting position, finally catching my breath while cradling my right hand to my chest. The fingers had gone blessedly numb, but I knew they would scream bloody murder at me if I so much as bumped them. I'd broken toes before, and they were the worst. Every twitch of a muscle could set them off as if you'd just broken them again. I had a feeling the fingers would be the same.

Leaning over to Ethan, careful to use only my left hand, I pulled my flashlight from my pack that he still carried. The flickering beam showed us a space that was as different from the hallway above as I could have thought possible, with the exception of the darkness.

Bars covered the walls in every direction,

obvious windows and doors set into along the length of the hall. Over each door was etched words.

"Oh, this is . . . this is bad," Ethan breathed out, his head swiveling as he took in the signs.

There were no sounds, no warning of danger coming. "Why? And be specific. Not some random 'we're in a jail made for supernaturals, what isn't bad?' kind of thing," I said.

Ethan lifted his wand and used it to light the area more, highlighting a word not in any language I knew. But I could feel it in my belly, like a sound, more than a proper word.

"Berserker," Ethan said. "That's what that word is. And it's on every single cell door. This is where they house all the shifters that go mad. They're usually killed very soon after being brought in here, if they don't come back from the madness."

I did a slow turn, breathing in through my nose and picking up on the faint scent of animals, shit, and body funk. I wrinkled my face up. "But this is where Pete is. He hasn't gone berserker."

"Why couldn't I smell this when I was hanging up there?" Gregory said. "I should have been able to. I really wasn't that far away."

Ethan grunted. "We broke through the spell

that kept your section separate from this one. When we all fell, that is. But when I was climbing down to you two, I saw a platform to one side with a door in the wall. I think that's where we were supposed to come in."

"You're sure about the berserker thing here? That there won't be any others in here?" I threw the questions out, kind of half-heartedly.

"Of course I'm sure," he snapped.

I held up a hand. "Old Ethan, go away, bring back new Ethan, please."

Gregory snickered, though I heard the tension in him despite the laughter. "If only it were that easy."

Sweeping the area, I let the bond between Pete and me pull me forward. "Watch for traps."

Ethan stepped up beside me. "I doubt there are too many in this hall." He pulled out the map he'd stolen from his father and held it out.

"Why is that?" Gregory asked. "Wait, you got a cheat sheet again?"

I noted that Gregory hadn't said anything about Colt. It would come soon enough—I doubted he'd just take my word for it about Colt—but right then, I was glad he wasn't pressing a confrontation.

Ethan shot him a look before glancing back at me. "This floor was protected from above. That big hallway you and I passed through? It's the main strip through the prison. All the different sections branch out from it." He flipped through the papers to the one showing the bottom levels of the prison. "Look. This is the Hall of Shifters. See, no protections here."

My guts twisted at the implication. The shifters themselves were the literal monsters we'd have to deal with.

Gregory and Ethan either picked up on my thoughts or came to that conclusion on their own.

"So, berserker shifters? Great," Gregory grumbled. "Long as we stay quiet, we should be able to get to Pete."

I nodded. Simple. Straightforward. "Here's the way." I pointed to the left of the main hall. Picking up speed, I winced as my jog jiggled my fingers. Holding them tightly to my chest, I kept moving. We had to hurry.

To the left of us a low growl came from behind a metal door with slats in it. We pressed to the right only to have something hit the door we were up against with a rage-filled roar. Back and forth we went, our fear only ramping up and seeming to feed into the beasts. "I thought you said—"

"Obviously I was wrong," Ethan panted out, sweat beading his face. "It's like they're infecting us to be more afraid."

"We're prey," Gregory said as he pressed against my leg. "They are the predators. It's normal to be scared of things that want to eat you."

While I felt the edges of the fear that the berserkers were inflicting on us, I was more focused on the task at hand.

God only knew what Ash and Nicholas were up to.

Or Frost and her crew. It was slowly freaking me out that both groups had been fairly quiet.

I stopped in front of a wooden door on my left, the iron bands holding it to the wall shiny and bright. New.

The wood smelled fresh cut. "Everything here is new."

"Maybe the shifter who was in here before broke out," Ethan said.

Gregory and I gave him a look, and he shrugged. "Just saying."

"How about not just saying," Gregory snapped. "How about shutting your piehole?"

I put a hand to the door, and like the main prison door it opened easily. As if welcoming us in. I grimaced. "Pete?" He was here, not far in, either. "Pete, come on, man."

A low snarl rippled through the air, and there was the scratch of claws on stone as he scrabbled toward me. I reached back and slammed the door shut, keeping us both in the small space.

Honey badger Pete was seriously badass.

And he was pissed.

"Pete!" I hollered as I dodged his first swipe.

"He's gone. They've forced him into being a berserker somehow!" Ethan barked through the door.

"No shit, Sherlock!" Gregory yelled. "Don't hurt him, Wild! We have to try and bring him back!"

I pinned my back against the wall and kept my flashlight directly in Pete's eyes. There was definitely nobody home in there. But the light in his eyes kept him from seeing me easily.

Snarling and swiping with his wicked claws, he came at me again, and I pushed him back with the tip of my boot.

That was a bad idea.

His head snaked sideways, and he grabbed hold of my ankle, dragging me to the ground, shaking me like a honey badger with a bone. I didn't dare pull a knife. I didn't want to hurt him. "Pete, snap the hell out of it!"

A deeper snarl, and I wished for nothing more than a Snickers bar to throw at him.

Wait.

"Ethan, in my bag there are two Snickers bars! Throw them in!"

I had no idea if he'd heard me over the snarling and growling of honey badger Pete. For just a moment, I heard his thoughts, and that didn't make me feel any better.

Kill it. Eat it. Kill it. Eat it.

"No, Pete, no eating me!" I pushed at him with my free boot, and he latched onto the sole of it, yanking me back and forth across the floor, dragging me along with him as if I weighed nothing. "Hurry it up, Ethan!"

"Here!" Two chocolate bars were tossed onto the floor, just out of reach. I scrabbled for them, my fingers brushing against one package before Pete could dig deeper into my boot. His teeth were already pressing against my skin.

I twisted hard onto my belly, gritting my teeth as my broken fingers banged into the ground. "Son of a bi—" I slapped my hands over the chocolate bar and pulled it to my mouth, using my teeth to rip the package open. "Pete!"

I leaned forward, holding the bar out to him, my good hand dangerously close to his snarling face. He froze, his teeth still sunk through my boot, but his nose twitched. I waved the chocolate bar back and forth in front of his nose. "Come on, buddy. This is much better than a stinking old boot."

Another nose twitch. He slowly released my boot and then lunged for the chocolate bar. Taking it all in one bite. I yelped and scrambled backward, grabbing the second bar and peeling it open quickly. "Come on, buddy."

He waddled toward me, his thoughts changing as they touched my mind.

Snickers . . . give it to me.

"Only if you promise to shift back."

He grunted, and I held out the second bar. It would have to be enough for now. I hoped.

Honey badger Pete took the second bar a little slower than the first, chewing it up in three bites instead of one. I slid back slowly until I was against the door, then pushed to my feet.

Honey badger Pete tipped his head slowly at me.

I'm going to shift. You got clothes?

"Of course." I fumbled for the door and stepped out, backing right into Ethan. "In my bag, there is a pair of pants and a shirt."

Ethan's eyebrows worked up. "The chocolate bars worked?"

"Snickers satisfies," Gregory said.

"Hey," Pete called out, "I can hear you."

I grinned, though I was still shaking a little. I could feel it in my guts that it had been closer than even Pete realized. A few minutes more and we wouldn't have been able to bring him back. If we'd taken the longer route . . . "Toss him the clothes."

Ethan did just that, shoving the clothes through the door. A few moments later, Pete shuffled out. He wasn't as chubby as he'd been even the day before, and the clothes fit him not too badly, all things considered.

He didn't lift his eyes, though, staring hard at the floor. "Sorry about that."

I threw an arm across his shoulders. "Don't even worry about it. Will you be okay for a bit now?"

He nodded. "They pushed me into it. I . . . don't remember much after they snagged us off the street." Pete narrowed his eyes as he lifted his head. "But you, I remember. You helped your father and his buddies take us. Wally said you killed Colt!"

Ethan paled, and I stepped between them. "Wait. He's with us, Pete. Really with us. His father had a spell on him that forced him to kill Colt."

"You're just saying that because you kissed him," Gregory said, and I turned to him.

Oh, this I did not need. Then another thought hit me. "Wait, you can tell who I kiss?"

Gregory shrugged. "Whatever the bond is between us, it's been filtering through memories. I caught a glimpse of you kissing him, though it did seem to be more one-sided than he would have liked."

I groaned and held my hands up. "Can we discuss this later?"

"No," Pete growled, and I realized he was jonesing on his honey badger badassery. I sighed.

"I kissed him in order to dig into his memories, to see if we could trust him. And we can." I put a hand on Pete's shoulder, holding him back. "Pete, if you trust me, then you can trust Ethan."

"And what if he showed you what he wanted to show you?" Gregory said as he turned toward

Ethan. "What if . . . shit, I want to trust you, Wonder Bread. Despite everything."

That he was using my nickname for Ethan was almost touching. Almost.

Ethan frowned. "But?"

"But can you deny that the power struggle between our two houses isn't an issue? That my house is a slave to yours in pretty much every sense of the word?" Hurt flowed beneath Gregory's words, and while this really wasn't the time . . . I also didn't know if there would be a good time.

I needed them working together, with me, not against each other.

So, I stepped back. "Okay, boys, have your say. You've got five minutes. Make it count."

Hardest thing I ever had to do was see the three of them square off and not try to fix this between them. Ethan took a deep breath. "You're right, Gregory. And I was raised to see all the houses as less than the House of Wonder. I don't know how I can convince you that a lot of how I acted was pushed on me. To keep myself safe."

Pete drew in a deep breath. "He doesn't smell like he's lying."

Gregory put his hands on his hips, like a miniature Peter Pan. "What about your father?"

"I cut ties with him." His hand drifted to his shoulder, where he'd taken away the spell that had controlled him. "Wild is right. I didn't want to hurt Colt. My father . . . the best way to describe it is like being a puppet. I had no say in what happened."

Pete and Gregory were quiet for a good twenty seconds.

"I'm satisfied. You smell okay." Pete held out his hand. "Welcome back."

Gregory, though, was not so easily swayed. "I'll take it, for now. But don't think I won't be watching you."

Ethan nodded at him. "Fair enough."

Seriously, where had *this* Ethan been? If this had been the Ethan I'd first met, maybe things would be different . . . nope. Seriously no, I was not going there.

"Let's move," I said. "Orin and Wally are waiting."

19

Finding Orin wasn't quite as easy as I'd hoped, though he was closer to us than Wally.

At the end of the Hall of Shifters, there was a single doorway leading out. Pete was on my left, and he put his hand to the door and leaned in. "Yeah, this smells like the way out. Or at least, it's where I can retrace my scent, so they brought me in this way for sure."

"Good deal." I nodded for him to take the lead. "You first, me, then Gregory. Ethan, you bring up the rear."

They all moved to take their positions. "You normally take the rear guard," Gregory said. "Why the change?"

"Because I trust him, and I'm hurt," I said. "We have to be smart. It's not smart for me to be in a guard position when I'm not one hundred percent."

That brought them all to a standstill, the three of them turning to look at me. I held up my hand, the two fingers swollen and purpling already. "I'm down one hand." My dominant hand at that, which really blew chunks.

Ethan grabbed my shoulder. "Damn it, Wild. I could have helped with that. I'm no Mara, but I could have lessened the injury. Now . . . I can't do anything. You'd need a more experienced healer to re-break the bones and heal them properly."

Damn indeed. "Next time," I said. Because yeah, there would be a next time, and we all knew it.

"Go on," I said. "We have to hurry."

"The door is locked," Pete said.

"I got it. Less magic is better, I think." Gregory moved up beside him and fiddled with the handle of the door, using only his fingers, until there was a pop of a lock opening.

"How did you do that?" I asked.

Gregory shrugged. "Something opened up in me when the Shadowkiller took you. The House of

Unmentionables used to have a great connection to metals and the earth. I can feel the metal now, and manipulate it to some degree. I'm sure that's why they wrapped me in the chains back there. To see what I could do."

"You didn't do anything," Ethan pointed out.

Gregory shot him a look. "And they left me alone. I'm not an idiot, Ethan. The more you show them, the more they want from you."

Like a test, to see if his magic would open up like Wally's had.

I thought about Ash, about how the earth had heaved and shifted at his command. Ash was connected to a Chameleon too. Was that the key? Was it my connection to my crew that was opening us all to different abilities?

Pete stepped it up, opening the door and breaking into a jog. Pete, running without complaint. I knew why, though I didn't say. His worry for Wally was at the forefront of his emotions.

He followed his nose, pausing here and there, but mostly keeping up the pace, and we followed him. This section of the prison had rougher walls, made of solid dark gray concrete, and while there were doors, they didn't draw Pete.

Our footsteps echoed back to us, but there was no other sound.

No, that wasn't true. A steady thump of something was at the edge of my hearing. I couldn't tell if it was machinery or what, but it came from deep within the prison. "You picking up on that, Pete?" I asked.

"Yes," he whispered back. "Any ideas?"

"No, so just keep moving."

While he didn't pick up speed, he didn't slow either, which was good.

The feeling of Orin got closer, almost as if he were right there, standing beside me, and my feet slowed of their own volition.

"Orin is close," I said.

Pete held up his hand, and we came to a stop. "Another doorway. I can't smell him, but it's where they brought me through."

I blinked and looked upward. If I could see through the concrete, I was sure I'd be looking right at our vampire friend. "Let's hope it's stairs."

Once more Gregory moved the metal parts inside the lock and slid the door open. No alarms went off. "This is a really weird prison," I said. "No guards that I've seen. Traps, yes. Danger, yes. But that's not a prison . . . that's . . ."

Ethan held out the map, showing us where we stood. "Is it a prison? Yes and no. If everyone was just in cages next to each other, they'd talk, maybe even form alliances. Maybe even break out together. Keeping the different houses apart is how they keep them weak."

"They?"

Ethan shot me a look. "The leaders of our world. The heads of state if you want to call them that."

What he said seemed to echo between us. "That's always been the goal, hasn't it?" I said.

"Of Frost and the House of Wonder, of the Culling Trials even. To keep everyone else weak."

Gregory gave a slow nod. "Which is why they encourage rivalry between houses from the earliest age on. Much as Ethan has repeatedly proved my point that the House of Wonder produces the most egotistical bastards . . . I was taught to hate mages from an early age." He shrugged as if it didn't matter, but there was a measure of shame in him as he spoke. Small, but it was there.

"And the belief that one is better than the others," Ethan added, shaking his head. "That was all I learned. That the other houses were all lesser. That they needed to be ruled."

A low laugh rumbled from behind us, and we whipped around, facing the dark concrete hall. The door was still open, and I peered through it into murky darkness.

The laugh faded and a voice followed us. "You think you're so smart."

I blinked. "I know that voice. Barnaby?" Oh, shit. "Go, go, he's a mostly starved vampire. With a dead ram!"

The clatter of said ram's hooves on the cement had me scrambling to get through the door with the guys. We slammed it shut just as the creepy ram skeleton crashed into the base of it, pushing all three of us back a few steps.

"Push!" I yelled as I hit the door with my shoulder, using my own body weight against that stupid ram.

The door inched closed.

Fingers reached through the gap, wrapping around the edge of the door. "Harder!" I hollered.

Ethan stepped back and pointed his wand at the fingers. "*Bravisium*!"

His wand shot something dark green at the skeletal hands, and they yanked back. The weight lifted from the door, and we slammed it shut. "Gregory, can you jam the lock?"

"On it!" His fingers worked over the lock, and a moment later he stepped back.

Something heavy—most likely the undead ram—hit the door again, and the center of it bowed toward us.

I took a step back. "Time to go."

I turned and found myself staring at a damn ladder that went straight up. "Pete, how did they get you down here?"

"No idea. I was blindfolded and zap strapped, but I don't remember a ladder," he grumbled, but he went straight for the bottom rungs and started climbing.

The door boomed again with another hit. "Hinges are going," Gregory said.

"Hurry up, go, go." I pushed them ahead of me. Ethan paused, and I shook my head. "Go."

The three of them scrambled up the ladder, and I waited at the bottom, watching the door bow inward with another hit, the sound of the metal screeching as it loosened. Could I kill Barnaby? Maybe. But with my fingers broken, it would be dicey. We needed a better option.

I blinked a few times. Wally had gotten

stronger under the Shadowkiller's attack. So had Gregory.

What if all of their abilities had ramped up?

"We need Orin," I said, turning and leaping partway up the ladder before taking hold of a rung with my good hand and scrambling upward. I didn't know how I knew. My head and instinct said to get to our vampire, and he'd deal with Barnaby.

Even with a head start and only one good hand, I caught up to Ethan and the guys. Because they weren't moving. "What's the holdup?"

"Trapdoor," Pete barked down, and a laugh circled up to us.

"You can't escape me now, and I get to eat all of you!"

This was not how I wanted to end my week.

"Ethan or Gregory, now's the time!" I looked up to see Gregory climb up and over Pete's back, hanging off him as he worked on the lock. "It's a spell holding it, not metal," he reported. There was shuffling above me as they changed positions and a few curses thrown between Gregory and Ethan.

I looked down the ladder in time to see a pair of glowing red eyes staring straight back. Barnaby opened his mouth, and his fangs picked up the dim light.

"Can't get worse," I muttered.

A loud clang rippled upward, and the ladder shuddered underneath us.

"Holy cats, what's happening now?" Pete hollered.

"Ram skeleton," I yelled back as Barnaby got close enough to make a grab for my legs. I kicked out, catching him in the face. He swung out into open space but didn't let go of the rung. Instead, he dangled for a moment and then snapped back to the ladder as if he were made of elastic bands and not barely held together rags and bones.

He snapped his teeth. "Yummy, yummy."

"How did you even get here?" I kicked out, but he dodged the blow.

"I have friends in high places," he whispered, his eyes fading to a solid black. "They brought me here to find you. And drain every last drop of your lovely blood."

"Nope, not today." I twisted around so my back was against the ladder and my left hand wrapped around the side. Dragging my knees to my chest, I waited for him to get closer. One boot to the face hadn't worked.

Maybe two would.

"Ethan, hurry your ass up!"

"Almost! The spell is heavy!"

Heavy, what the hell did that even mean? I focused on the vampire lunging up at me. Waiting for him to make a stupid move. And a starving vampire would. I just had to make sure I was ready. And maybe I could hurry it up.

"You want to bite me?" I purred down at him.

"Yes," he growled.

"Well, you can't. It's not appropriate for me to discuss biting in any sort of a way that could possibly be construed as sexual. Unless I said . . . bite me, you dumbass."

He snarled and let go of the ladder with both hands and pushed toward me, his remaining fingers outstretched to grab me. A blur of stinking death. A stupid move.

I kicked out with both feet, catching him in the chest and sending him flying out into space. His fingers raked down the outsides of my legs like hot pokers, and I hissed through the pain. But the pain was worth it. Barnaby fell ass over teakettle all the way down to the bottom of the ladder.

He howled as he fell, then went quiet when he hit the ground. His ram buddy limped around him, lifting that skull up and looking at me with his bleeding eye sockets.

Not creepy at all.

The only problem? It seemed that I'd really pissed him off rather than disabled him.

A starving, half-crazed, and now very angry vampire wanted to kill me.

He twisted around to stare up the ladder . . . and smiled.

20

"I got it!" Ethan yelled at the same time Barnaby all but flew up the ladder toward me, mouth wide open like a shark going for a seal.

I climbed backward as fast as I could, eyes locked on the incoming vampire. My legs burned, my fingers ached, and just as I was starting to think we wouldn't make it, I was grabbed from above and dragged through a circular thick metal trapdoor.

It boomed shut as my feet cleared, and I sat there on the ground, breathing hard as Ethan wove a spell over the trapdoor. "That should keep it shut." The pride in his voice was no small thing.

I barely took note though as my eyes adjusted

to the dim light that spread out over the room full of tables. Tables? Was it some sort of classroom? Somehow, I doubted that.

Around the edges of the room, candles lit the space, and for just a brief moment, I thought we were clear of vampires in general. Until I realized what the tables actually were.

"Oh shit," Gregory breathed out. "Wild . . . we're in the catacombs, I think."

Catacombs.

Coffins.

Vampires.

Sure, there hadn't been any loose shifters in with Pete, but call me crazy, I didn't think we'd get that lucky again.

Fear spiked through the four of us, circling around and around and ramping up with each pass.

"Everybody take a deep breath and chill out," I said. "We get Orin, and we get the hell out of here."

"Agreed," the other three said in unison.

I pushed to my feet, wincing, but following the pull toward Orin. He wasn't far. I stopped in front of a coffin that wasn't even locked. "Help me," I said as I tucked my good hand under the lip and lifted with my legs. Ethan, Gregory, and Pete all got hold of the lid.

"Seriously, are they all this heavy?" Pete gasped out. "Cats on fire, this is ridiculous!"

I didn't disagree, but if there was no lock and the vampires were weak, a heavy lid would do the trick to keep them trapped inside.

Slowly we pushed the lid up, stopping about halfway. I could just see Orin's pale face and wide, staring eyes. But there was no reaction to my face being in his line of vision. "I can't go farther! I'm on my toes!" Gregory yelped.

He wasn't the only one who couldn't lift more. Already the strain was like nothing I'd ever felt before. Almost like the lid was getting heavier. I blinked and looked at it. "Ethan, can things be spelled to get heavier?"

"Yes," he growled the word.

I tucked my shoulder under the edge. "Gregory, can you pull Orin out?"

Ethan mimicked me, setting the lid on his shoulder. "Pete, help him! I can't do anything about this spell, but if we let go now, it will shut for good. We won't have another chance!"

"Seriously?" I yelped as the lid pushed down on me. "You could have said that earlier!"

"I didn't know until I felt it get heavy," he snapped.

Breathing through the shaking of my muscles and the protesting of my body in general, I watched as Gregory climbed into the coffin and pulled Orin partway out. The lid pushed downward, narrowing the gap.

"Hurry," I said. I was saying that word a lot, but there was no other choice.

Monsters behind us.

Monsters ahead.

And we still had to find Wally and fight our way back out to the alicorns. Preferably without coming across Frost herself.

Pete grabbed Orin under the arms and pulled. "Why isn't he awake? Orin, wake up!"

A terrible thought rippled through me. What if Orin had been killed? Was a truly dead vampire more controllable?

Pete and Gregory all but fell backward, pulling Orin with them. Ethan and I stepped away at the same time, and the lid clanged shut, shuddering the coffin and the ground around us. I went to my knees, breathing hard. "Has he got a pulse?"

Pete slid his fingers to Orin's neck and then

nodded. "Weak, but it's there. What are you thinking?"

I slid closer to Orin so I could see his very pale face up close. "He needs blood. That's my guess."

"Blood?" Pete tipped his head. "You think that he's—"

I shrugged. "I don't know, I just . . . it makes sense." I mean, I had enough scratches and cuts that giving Orin a little of my blood was no big deal. Not really.

The cut across my left forearm from the car crash had partially scabbed over, and it took just a flick of my fingernails to open it back up again. I squeezed the edges of the cut while I held it over Orin's mouth.

The thing was, I didn't know if it would work. But it was kind of like Orin's version of a Snickers bar, so why not?

A drop fell right in, and his eyes bugged open the second it touched his tongue. He gasped, his eyes looking straight at me. "Wild. It's a trap!"

I leaned back as Orin sat up. "I figured as much. We have to get Wally, though. We can't leave her."

His long, thin fingers grabbed at my arms. "No, we have to leave her."

I shook my head. "Not going to happen, Orin. Any more than I would have left you, or Ethan, or Gregory, or Pete."

Orin slumped and slowly let go of me. "Sorry. That . . . that was some of the instructions they left in me. Like they wanted me to drag you out." He ran a hand over his eyes. "I don't even know exactly, but I was supposed to stop you somehow."

"They?" Now it was my turn to grab a hold of him. "Who is they?"

"The master vampires," he said. "They want Wally. They think they can double cross Frost."

Around us the sound of groaning hinges sent a river of frustration through me. I stood, wobbled and then offered my hand to Orin. "Talk while we run. Unless you can stop an old, starving vampire?"

Orin shook his head. "Not yet. I don't think."

I pointed at Pete. "Keep a nose out for anything that will want to kill us. I'll lead. Everyone on their toes."

I locked onto the feeling of Wally in my head and twisted around until I found a doorway leading out. A simple doorway.

I ran toward it, hoping it was open like so many of them had been. The knob was firm in my hand.

Without even asking, Gregory and Ethan took a look at it. Both shook their heads.

"Not a spell," Ethan said.

"And not a metal I can deal with," Gregory said.

I swallowed hard. "Wally is on the other side, not far."

While I fumbled with the lock, Orin began to speak.

"They didn't want just you, Wild. Though you are the one that Frost wants for sure. They want . . . they want all of us, I think. And in order to get us all together, to show off our abilities they put us in here."

Part of my mind was on what he was saying, the other part on the door in front of me. "They didn't get enough at the Culling Trials?"

"The Culling Trials—as dangerous as it became, it was never the real world. This is. The Culling Trials was like an entry test to see who sparked the magic around them. We all sparked. A great deal if the efforts they are going to here are any indication."

I was on my knees, my good hand on the door-knob, the sounds of coffins opening behind me. "Orin, you have to slow them down!"

"I'll try." He did not sound confident.

I stared at the door. "What I wouldn't give for a key right about now."

Ethan crouched beside me and held out his hand. "I mean, the chances of it working are . . . well, Wally would know. But I'd say pretty bad in general."

The key in Ethan's hand was my key. Tommy's key. I scooped it up and gave him a look.

"Wally dropped it on the pier," he said. "I picked it up and meant to give it back to her."

"It won't work, there's no way," I said.

"Wally said it was a death key," Gregory pointed out. "That is something special in the House of Night, apparently. Why wouldn't it work?"

I looked over my shoulder to see three vampires standing still next to their coffins—apparently their lids hadn't been the heavy sort. I did a double blink. One of the vampires was Jared.

Jared was Orin's previous trainer.

"Orin?"

He had his hands out to the sides of his body and I could have sworn that a dark green mist rolled around him. "They can't see us right now. I'm blocking them."

"Badass," Pete said. "We are a bunch of badass cats!"

I turned back to the door even as a wave of panic hit me. I felt the others gasp and bit back on the urge to run.

"The same as before," Ethan grunted. "Like they are trying to scare us forward."

I flipped the key over.

"He's holding them back still, but I think you should move faster," Pete said.

Really, the worst that could happen was that we'd stuff the key in, and it wouldn't work. Right?

Deep breath in, pushing back the fear that crawled all over me, I shoved the key into the lock. The resistance was immediate.

"Won't work," I said.

Ethan put his hand on mine and his magic crawled over my skin and into the key. It went in a little further. "Gregory, Pete, we need you."

Gregory was next and when his magic slid over us the key sunk in further yet. The same with Pete. Each layer of magic helped the key fit better.

"Orin!" I looked over my shoulder and he met my eyes.

"If I let them go . . ."

"You have to, it's the only way," I said.

His shoulder straightened and then he dropped his hold on the other vampires and shot toward us. His hand latched on tight and the key sunk all the way in.

Bodies slammed against us, Ethan hollered as he was dragged backward and I cranked the handle to the right, yanked the key out, and stumbled through the door, the guys right behind me.

Ethan was wrestling with one of the vampires. Orin snaked a hand outward, threw the vampire off Ethan and jerked him through the door with us.

"Lock it!" Pete yelped.

I jammed the key back in the keyhole, the skull pressing against my palm as it clicked, and the lock slid home.

Still on my knees, I looked over my shoulder.

"Wally!" She was on the floor of the windowless, doorless room, seemingly asleep.

Pete reached her first, carefully pulling her into his lap. "She's . . . her heartbeat is really slow. Slower than Orin's was." His eyes shot to mine. "Wild, is she dying?"

I crouched next to her and took one of her hands in my good one. The room immediately softened, and two ghosts came into view.

One was Tommy, the other was my mother. I focused on Tommy first as he seemed the more solid of the two. Not that my mom wasn't a draw, but I needed current information.

"A little help here would be amazing," I said as I pushed some of my energy into Wally. Whatever was draining her was going to have to go through me first.

Tommy crouched next to me. "Your vampire friend is right. The master vampires want her—they want her as a vampire, because she is such a strong necromancer. Just like each of the houses want the other members of your crew. You were the key to them finding their abilities, Wild. But now . . ."

I stared hard at him as Wally slowly came around, muttering under her breath.

"Fifteen percent of people who drown do so . . . eighty-six out of every hundred who face a boa constrictor . . . one percent chance of survival against a T-Rex . . ." She curled against Pete, who blushed rapidly but didn't let her go as she mumbled into his chest.

Smart guy.

"Keys. Everything is about the keys," my mom said and I looked to her.

"What do you mean?"

Behind us, the door rattled. "Pick her up, Pete." I kept a hand on Wally, and Pete did as I asked, his face going a bit redder, but he was strong enough. I was sure of it.

My mother looked us over. "You have one of them. There is a place where they all fit. Five houses. Five keys. The sickness that is raging . . . it is tied to these keys. You have very little time, Wild." Her smile was sad. "Your father has this sickness. Every null has this sickness. It has been spreading slowly, but a new strain has been developed. One meant to change our world and reshape it . . . there is very little time before there is no chance to reverse it. Tommy died trying."

Chills rippled through me. How did she know this? This was the task that Tommy had been after, this was what got him killed.

"You cannot trust him," my mom whispered, looking over her shoulder at something I couldn't see. "He is tied to another—"

The walls around us rippled and were torn apart with a shriek of metal screeching, beams twisting, and tile shattering. The six of us crouched together, unintentionally touching one another, and there was a surge of power between us.

Alone, we could be taken down, pulled apart and made into people we weren't.

Together we were beyond strong.

I stood and turned, my crew at my back. The dust settled around us, tinkling down with bits and pieces of mortar.

Across from me stood Frost, her hands tucked behind her back as she surveyed us. Her hair was a bright blond now, her eyes the same icy blue. She'd been over eighty when I'd met her, but draining the lives of kids had made her younger.

Now she wasn't much older than me.

"You were right. The fear drove them and yet they still completed the tasks at hand. I believe even I could learn something from them." She snapped her fingers. "Excellent idea, Nicholas, to bring them here. Of course, it is disappointing how easily she fell for the ruse. Then again, brains were never a strong suit for Shades." Her lips curved down.

Time slowed as I turned to see Nicholas step up beside her. His gaze didn't meet mine.

Ethan growled. "I knew we shouldn't trust him!"

Hindsight was a real bitch.

"What do you want to do with them now?" Nicholas asked softly. Subservient. But no Ash, the gargoyle was missing.

Slowly from the shadows we were joined by others of what I assumed were Frost's crew. A white gargoyle. A lion shifter. A necromancer and a vampire. And for the House of Wonder? Helix himself. Each went to stand behind one of my crew.

She clapped her hands together. "I will bind the others to me, then give them to their masters. The last thing we need is a third Chameleon running loose. The amount of power they have together will sustain me for years." She laughed. "We have let her stay free long enough. It is time to break her."

Nicholas turned and flicked his wand at me, picking me up as if I were nothing. Just like in the House of Wonder.

I twisted around to see my five friends pushed by someone from each of their houses down to their knees, necks held in harsh hands. I could not let this happen. Because if I did, I had no doubt that not only would my friends be hurt even worse, but my family would be next. My sister. My brother.

My dad.

"I am sorry, niece," Nicholas said as he deposited me at Frost's feet, forcing me to my knees, the same as my friends.

With everything I had, I lurched upward so I stood and stared her in her face, rage and a healthy dose of fear driving me, pumping my blood and giving me strength.

"You will *never* break me."

Her smile was nothing short of wicked as she reached out and grabbed me by the chin, her power sinking into me. I locked my knees, and her hand tightened until the bones in my jaw ached.

"That is exactly what your brother said . . . right before I killed him."

HiJinks Ink Publishing
www.shannonmayer.com

Mayer, Shannon
Shadowspell Academy: Year of the Chameleon, Book 5

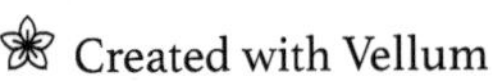

UP NEXT!

ABOUT THE AUTHOR

Check out all my links to keep up to date, and my website for what's happening!

www.shannonmayer.com

or my newsletter for extra sneak peeks!

NEWSLETTER